...eral ... ...ing water below. ... fe thrill and an amazing ... ...ir faces and get as close to Niagara Falls as they could without being in real danger.

Not to die.

With the roar of the falls and Graham's nervous outburst ringing in her ears, Sydney struggled, her poncho making squeaking noises as it chafed against the railing.

After several seconds of intense struggle, he reached his left hand around Sydney's throat, his fingers squeezing hard. *He's going to strangle me!* Sydney thought in a panic as her eyes blinked out rapid tears. The sound of the water was deafening. Blood rushed to Sydney's head as her neck fell farther back, her long blond hair dangling over the water.

Sydney gulped for air as her attacker wrapped both of his hands more tightly around her neck, shaking her. He pushed her against the slick wet railing, and it groaned with their weight. A half-formed sob came out as Sydney realized she had only a handful of seconds of air left. Soon she would be unconscious.

Then he'll toss me like a doll into the rapids. . . .

ALIAS™

FREE FALL

AN ORIGINAL PREQUEL NOVEL BASED ON THE

HIT TV SERIES CREATED BY J. J. ABRAMS

CHRISTA ROBERTS

BANTAM BOOKS

NEW YORK ✷ TORONTO ✷ LONDON ✷ SYDNEY ✷ AUCKLAND

Alias: Free Fall

A Bantam Book / January 2004
Text and cover art copyright © 2004 by Touchstone Television

ISBN: 0-553-49405-8

Visit us on the Web! www.randomhouse.com

Published simultaneously in the United States and Canada

Bantam Books is an imprint of Random House Children's Books, a
division of Random House, Inc. BANTAM BOOKS and the rooster
colophon are registered trademarks of Random House, Inc.

PRINTED IN THE UNITED STATES OF AMERICA

OPM 10 9 8 7 6 5 4 3 2 1

ALIAS™

FREE FALL

"DOES IT GET ANY better than this?" Francie Calfo let out a contented sigh, gazing out at the crashing Pacific surf. A summer party anthem was playing on the radio, the sun beat brightly in the cloudless blue sky, and the smell of coconut-scented suntan lotion wafted through the air.

Sydney Bristow settled back in her striped blue beach chair and cracked open a wet can of Sprite. "Only if I had someone here with a tall glass of ice—and a fan."

Francie tilted her head toward a group of guys

playing volleyball on the sand. "I'm sure that can be arranged."

"Mmm, sorry, they look way too involved in their game." Sydney picked up the paperback novel she'd stuffed into her canvas beach bag. This was the first day she and Francie had spent together at the beach in weeks, and she was glad that it was just the two of them. "I've been dying to read this."

Francie looked over at the book. "*Middlemarch*?" She scowled. "Have you ever heard of a beach read?" She gestured to the lively scene around them. "Syd, for the first time in months, we are free! No more studying, no more finals, no more all-nighters. Come on! Can't you stop being responsible and vegetate for just an hour? You make the rest of us look way too shallow and vacuous." She grinned. "See, I wasn't sleeping through English lit the whole semester."

It was hard to believe their first year of college was over. Back in September, Sydney had been a scared, clueless freshman. The UCLA campus had seemed dauntingly huge, the classrooms and dorms filled with intimidating strangers, and the workload overwhelming. Not to mention that only a few weeks into the school year, she'd been secretly recruited by SD-6, a covert branch of the CIA based in Los Angeles. She had gone from frightened kid to a full-fledged secret agent dedicated to protecting the United States against all enemies, foreign and domestic. To say that freshman year had been an adjustment was putting it mildly.

Sydney took a sip of cold soda. But now, ten months later, things were completely different. She knew where to park and which professors were notoriously difficult. She knew which campus cafeteria ladies were grumpy and that the best place to study was on the second floor of the health sciences library. She knew that having a roommate could be completely exasperating and totally perfect (especially when said roommate came home with a new outfit and let you wear it before she did).

But most of all, Sydney had learned about herself. Being an agent for the United States government was more than just a job. She hated lying to her friends, but the fact that the CIA trusted her to go on missions for her country, trusted her with top-secret, life-and-death information, made Sydney feel on top of the world. It was an incredible responsibility. She'd been waiting all her life for a chance to make a difference. Now, after months of training and several successful missions, not only did she feel physically ready for any challenge, she felt mentally prepared as well.

That's what was making the summer ahead a bit of a bummer.

"You're doing it again," Francie accused, pointing a French-manicured nail at Sydney, startling her into dropping her book.

"What?"

Francie peered at her over the top of her white-framed sunglasses. "You know. Getting that distracted look on your face, like you just remembered you left your curling iron plugged in or a tray of cookies in the oven too long." She shook her head disapprovingly. "That is not allowed in summer, missy!"

Sydney laughed. "I know. I'm psyched about summer. Really."

Francie sighed. "You know, you have only yourself to blame. You could have gotten yourself a fun yet completely pointless summer job, like being a shot girl at one of those bars down on Sunset. Or—or becoming an extra on a movie set. You'd be perfect at that, with your classic looks. Or—"

"Or working full-time at Credit Dauphine because it's a good job and they offered me a nice chunk of change to pick up extra hours this summer," Sydney finished. She and Francie had had this discussion at least ten times. Francie couldn't understand why anyone would voluntarily work indoors, at a bank, when the beaches and outdoor cafes were beckoning. Sydney had a laundry list of excuses why the bank was the perfect place of employment.

Of course, the real reason wasn't on that list.

Not that she wasn't glad to work for SD-6 in the summer—she was. It would have been silly for her to even think of getting another job. Not only would the pay be much worse than what she earned as an agent, but there was no point in learning a new job only to quit two months later. All year long, Sydney had struggled to balance school and SD-6. Now she had only SD-6 to worry about. And that was a good thing, right?

It's not like I have anything else on my plate, she thought, closing her eyes for a moment. Her father had recently visited her in Los Angeles, and although there had been a few nice moments in between all the awkward ones, the whole thing had left her depressed.

They had never been close. Ever since Sydney's mother, Laura, had been killed in a car crash when Sydney was a child, Jack Bristow had stayed as far away from his daughter as possible. Her childhood was a blur of nannies and boarding school and more business trips than she could count. He didn't seem to want her in his life. Sometimes Sydney wondered if he wished she'd never been born at all.

Yet despite the ice-cold air that hung between them every time they were together, Sydney still held out some small nugget of hope that they could actually have a normal father-daughter relationship. Go to Athletics games . . . catch a movie . . . have dinner. And every time, her hopes were dashed. Even when they did spend time together, it was never like she hoped it would be. They were virtual strangers, growing more distant as the years passed. After this last visit, Sydney had resigned herself to the fact that they were just two very different people, with very different personalities. And that made her feel more unloved than ever.

As for romance, she'd ended things with Burke once and for all. Her on-again, off-again relationship with her UCLA classmate was off for good. He was a sweet, nice person, and it wasn't fair to string him along, never being able to be honest with him, never letting him feel like he could ever truly understand her. Not that Burke was eager to hang around her any longer. After Sydney had reluctantly told him about Noah, Burke had been understandably upset—and angry. He'd avoided her those last few days on campus. She'd heard from her friend Todd that Burke was going to Joshua Tree this summer to "find himself." Sydney hoped that he did find whatever he was looking for . . . and maybe meet someone who wouldn't have a secret life as part of the package.

At least with Noah Hicks, there weren't any secrets like that.

There wasn't any security, either. Sydney never knew quite where she stood with the older, more experienced SD-6 agent. Maybe that was why she liked him so much.

She watched now as a harried-looking mother chased her young son along the beach as he darted into the water. "I wouldn't exactly call your job glamorous," Sydney said to Francie, foraging in her bag for some suntan lotion. "Got it," she said at last, popping the top and rubbing some of the white lotion onto her legs. "Picking up after three rugrats, schlepping off to their summer home in New Mexico, and running after them twenty hours a day? Wow, you were lucky to get that one."

Francie pouted. "I am lucky! These aren't regular kids, you know. Their mother is one of the top food critics in L.A. And if I ever want to open my own restaurant, what better person—"

"To learn from," Sydney finished. Then she laughed. "I'm sure you'll be learning about all sorts of exotic cuisine. Peanut butter and jelly sandwiches, s'mores, Rice Krispies Treats . . ."

"Stop! You're making me hungry." Francie adjusted her tropical print bikini and reached over for the small nylon cooler they'd packed earlier that morning. "Okay, we've got fruit salad, pasta salad—"

"Any sandwiches?"

Sydney and Francie turned to see two tall, cute guys in board shorts standing at the end of their beach towels.

"If not, we've got our own," said one of them, his surfer blond hair falling across his face.

His friend gestured behind them. "See that red cooler over there? Totally stocked with food and water. We just wanted to make sure you girls had enough to eat."

Francie tilted her head. "Bet you don't have homemade chocolate cake."

Sydney raised her eyebrows. That cake was for the two of them to share! Francie must have thought these guys were really cute to offer up some of her most prized dessert.

A few moments later, the guys—Matt and David—had set up their things next to Sydney and Francie.

"So do you come to this beach often?" Matt asked Sydney, taking a big bite of pasta salad.

Sydney laughed. "Only when I want to have some peace and quiet and relax."

Matt clutched his tanned chest. "Ouch! Hey, if I'm bugging you, just tell me."

Sydney shook her head. "No, you're not." Francie and David were totally hitting it off—in fact, they were feeding each other pretzels. And Matt seemed like a nice guy. He was cute enough, with his surfer hair, brown eyes, and toned build. It was just that, well, Sydney wasn't really open to meeting anyone. She wasn't even much interested in making platonic friends. Because she'd only have to lie to them. It was hard. *No one ever mentions how much lying you do when you become a CIA officer.*

The pager in Sydney's tote bag went off. *In fact, the lying never ends.*

"Don't even tell me!" Francie screeched as Sydney shot an apologetic look at Matt, then reached for her pager. She squinted to read the message on its small screen: SLOANE.

"I'm sorry, guys. I need to make a phone call."

"Why do they always do this?" Francie said, rolling her eyes. "Don't they know that it's summer? That you're still a teenager?" She shook her head in disgust. "Credit Dauphine rules your life!"

Francie gave a perplexed Matt and David an exasperated look. "The bank Sydney works at falls *completely* apart if she doesn't show up there on the weekends."

Sydney took out her cell phone and stood up, brushing some sand off her legs. "I'll be right back." She walked down to the ocean, letting the water cool her toes. Her phone looked just like a regular cell phone, but it worked worldwide and it couldn't be traced. Sydney used it to make cover calls to Francie—and to make sure she was accessible 24/7 to SD-6. Shielding her face from the sun, she punched in the number she'd memorized.

"Sydney! How are you?" came Arvin Sloane's confident voice over the line.

"Hello! I'm fine, thanks," she said, trying to quell the nerves that always seemed to jump inside her when she was speaking with her new handler at the agency. "Do you need me to come in?"

Sloane chuckled. "And miss this beautiful summer day? No, Sydney. I'm calling with an invitation."

Sydney blinked. An invitation?

"My wife, Emily, and I are having a dinner party later this evening. It's nothing extravagant, but I thought it might be a nice way for you to get to know me on a more personal level. See that we truly *are* one big family at SD-6." Sloane paused. "That is, of course, if you're free."

Sydney stared longingly over at Francie and their new friends, all of them laughing like crazy. She gave the splashing surf around her a long look, then took a deep breath.

"It sounds lovely. Of course I am."

2

"OKAY, YOU MADE IT. Now relax," Sydney told herself, closing the door to her white Mustang and walking up the fancy stone walk toward Arvin Sloane's house. By the time she had found a decent dress and stopped at a Mobil station to fill her almost empty gas tank, she'd had barely enough time to find her way to the address she'd scribbled down. She wasn't even sure what part of L.A. she was in, there had been so many twists and turns.

Sydney glanced back at her car, parked in a mammoth brick-paved driveway between a sleek black Mercedes and a coppery Jaguar. A few other cars—another Mercedes, an Audi, and a canary yellow Hummer—were there as well. The sun was just starting to set in the west now, and the cars were bathed in crimson. "Must be nice," she whispered, her sandals clicking on the smooth stones. In a town where what you drove was everything, the cars parked in the driveway gave Sydney a pretty good idea about who was waiting inside.

Probably not other college students.

Sloane's house wasn't a typical L.A.-style bungalow . . . it was a villa. It looked like a home that would be found in Tuscany, deep in the hills of Italy. Lush landscaping filled in the front grounds, and tiny spotlights lit up the olive trees and lavender bushes that lined the walkway. Sydney could make out burnt-orange gables along the roof, and large potted ferns graced the expansive entry steps.

Taking a deep breath, Sydney rang the doorbell. She could hear a soft *ding-dong* chime inside.

Walking out on Francie on their last Saturday night together before Francie started her nanny job did not go over well. "I'm sorry," Sydney had apologized earlier that evening back in the dorm. "One of the computers is down, and I'm, um, the only one they were able to reach who has clearance to fix it."

"Yeah, because anyone with any sense knows that it's Saturday night, and that means you're supposed to do something fun." Luckily, Francie and Sydney had had plans with a group of friends. . . . Francie would still have plenty of people to hang out with. But Sydney knew it wasn't quite the same.

"What's the name of that place you're going to?" Sydney had asked, leaning against the doorframe. Even though she knew it was an impossibility, there was a part of her that really, truly, thought that maybe she could still go. "Magee's? On Sunset? If I can get off early, I'll meet you guys there."

Francie had slipped on a pair of wedges and given her hair a final fluff. "Like I believe you. You always say that, but you never actually do it."

"I'll try." Sydney had given her an impulsive hug. "Really."

But the moment Francie had closed the dorm door behind her, Sydney had thrown a pair of strappy black sandals, a small black clutch, and a cosmetics bag into a backpack. "Okay, cell phone, directions, wallet," she had said, checking off the rest of what she was going to need. Then she'd slid off her Bugs Bunny watch and replaced it with a silver bangle Fossil one that she rarely wore. She hastily put some of Francie's yummy just-baked chocolate fudge brownies in a plastic container. "Everyone likes brownies, right?" she had said to herself before stepping out into the empty hallway. "Now it's time to go find a dress. This is one dinner party that I definitely can't be late to."

And I'm not late, she thought, glancing down at her watch. *In fact I'm right on—*

The door opened. A woman in a maid's uniform—starched black dress, white apron, flat black shoes—looked at her expectantly.

"Hi! I'm Sydney Bristow. I'm here for the dinner party?" she said tentatively, her eyes flicking upward to an ornate metal and crystal chandelier that hung in the high-ceilinged vestibule.

The maid smiled. "Come this way."

Sydney followed her down a long corridor, taking in the sumptuous surroundings. Beautiful oil paintings hung on the walls, hardwood floors gleamed from a fresh polish, and vases brimmed with meticulously arranged fresh flowers.

"They're out back," the maid explained as they walked through an ornate sitting room and stepped through French doors to a large flower-fringed patio and deck.

Small clusters of people stood about drinking wine. A tuxedoed waiter offered some canapés on a silver tray to a group of well-dressed women. Soft classical music played on outdoor speakers, and the smell of citronella candles drifted through the air.

"Have a good evening," the maid said, stepping back inside.

A few people glanced Sydney's way, gave her polite smiles, and then resumed their conversations. Sydney swallowed. She'd thought that maybe someone she knew from SD-6 might be here, like that nice Agent Dixon, or Graham, or maybe even Noah, but there wasn't a familiar face in sight. Not even Sloane's.

"Chianti, miss?" A man holding a tray of wineglasses had materialized beside her.

"Oh! Uh, sure," she said, taking one by the stem. Then she stared down at her hands. One gripped a glass of full Chianti very tightly. The other clutched a small plastic-wrapped container of . . . Francie's chocolate fudge brownies.

Sydney winced. How could she have thought that bringing *brownies* was a good idea? Back in the dorm it had seemed a nice gesture, but now, seeing these people, seeing this house—it just seemed completely amateurish. She watched as a man in an expensive-looking shirt tilted his head back and laughed, while the woman beside him smoked a long, narrow cigarette. They helped themselves to what looked like scallops wrapped in bacon. *Brownies. Why didn't I bring chocolate chip cookies and Kool-Aid while I was at it?* she thought miserably.

Sydney looked hastily around. No one would notice if she ditched the container inconspicuously in a potted fern, would they?

She was just about to do it when she felt someone touch her arm. *Great! Now I've practically been caught in the act of —*

"Welcome to our home," said the slender, pretty woman who stood at her side. She was wearing a blue satin Asian-style dress embroidered with flowers and a thin gold necklace with diamond-shaped crystals. Soft gold-tinged curls barely touched her shoulders, and her greenish gray eyes were warm and welcoming. "You must be Sydney," she said, leaning over to kiss Sydney on the cheek. She smelled like lilies.

"Yes," Sydney stumbled out, suddenly feeling a bit shy.

"I've heard such wonderful things about you," she said, taking Sydney's hand. "I'm Emily Sloane." Then she gestured down at the brownies. "Don't tell me you brought my absolute favorite dessert in the world," she said, her smile growing even wider.

Sydney's face relaxed into a huge smile too. "I—I guess I did," she said happily.

And in the few seconds they had spent together, Sydney already knew without a doubt that she was going to like this woman immensely.

3

LOS ANGELES TRAFFIC WAS its usual nightmare as Sydney cruised her Mustang along the highway toward the Credit Dauphine building Monday morning. She wore lightweight black pants with a sleeveless white knit shirt and a dab of clear lip gloss and mascara. Her straight brown hair was slicked into a long ponytail.

Francie hadn't even lifted her head from her pillow that morning to say good-bye.

As Sydney parked her car and walked through the underground lot, she could barely keep the spring out of her step. She didn't like lying about her new job, but there was no denying that being an agent-in-training with the CIA was the most exciting thing she'd ever done—not to mention the most important. And after that weekend, she felt completely energized.

The dinner at Sloane's villa couldn't have been any nicer. *Of course, that was because of the amazing Emily Sloane,* Sydney thought with a smile as she stepped into the elevator that would take her to SD-6's hidden headquarters on bank sublevel six. To Sydney's delight, Sloane's wife had taken her under her wing and introduced her to all the guests.

"Have you met Sydney?" Emily would say, approaching a cluster of people with that welcoming smile of hers, and soon Sydney found herself chatting about art exhibits and nature conservation with total strangers. Even though most of the guests were at least fifteen years older than she was, Emily had managed to find something about each of them that helped start a conversation with Sydney. But talking with Emily herself had turned out to be one of the best parts of the evening.

Sydney had been relieved to see that she was seated next to Emily at dinner. Long tables and cream-colored denim slipcovered chairs were set up under tents, and soft candlelight cast a warm, inviting glow over the outdoor "room." At first

Sydney had concentrated on saying and doing the right thing—Sloane had asked her not to talk about their jobs, and to maintain the cover of Credit Dauphine. But soon the notion of work had completely slipped away. There were much more interesting things to talk to Emily about.

Like the fact that she was an incredible chef! Sydney had been shocked to learn that instead of calling a caterer like everyone else did in L.A., Emily had prepared the entire meal herself, right down to the lobster bisque and the tender beef medallions that melted like butter in her mouth.

"I just like to cook," Emily had confessed as they ate. "I spent a good deal of time in southern Italy in my twenties, and somehow I never am able to stray far from the scent of olive oil and ripe Roma tomatoes." She laughed. "Of course, a nice glass of Merlot and Puccini in the CD player as I'm slicing and dicing make it even better."

Sydney thought it would be nice to chat with her about some of the places she had traveled to, but then decided she'd better not. It would be too easy to slip up—and too hard to explain how a college freshman like herself had traveled to France, Scotland, Hawaii, and New York—all during the school year.

And Sydney had never met anyone with such a

vast knowledge of music. Not only did Emily have every single Rolling Stones album ever released in the U.S., but they were all in mint condition. "You'll have to come over one day when Arvin's out and we can really blast it," Emily said when she found out Sydney was a huge fan of Mick and Keith. Her eyes twinkled. "Arvin is not one for rock."

"Sounds like a plan," Sydney had agreed, giggling at the thought. The cool thing was, she could tell that it wasn't an empty invitation—Emily really meant it.

"Sydney, dear, don't let Emily corrupt you with her musical taste," Sloane said teasingly from across the table. He pushed back the sleeves of his white linen shirt. "Frankly, I don't know what I'd do without earplugs." Her new handler had greeted her with a hug, insisting that she call him Arvin, and his laid-back, relaxed manner made Sydney realize just how fortunate she was to be under someone like him at the agency.

She marveled at the way Emily made sure everyone felt welcome. From keeping goblets filled with ice water to telling sidesplitting jokes to producing a new outfit for a guest who had spilled wine on her dress, Emily was the consummate hostess.

And she was a born listener. Emily was so attentive, and seemed so genuinely interested in what Sydney had to say, that by the time dessert was served, Sydney found herself spilling details about Burke and Noah and all the pressures of school, leaving out any SD-6-related specifics. Part of her felt kind of silly—someone of Emily Sloane's stature was light-years away from the kind of love traumas Sydney was having. *She's so confident and worldly. She's probably never had a romantic crisis in her life,* Sydney had thought admiringly, gazing at her in the candlelight as she laughed at something a guest had said.

But Emily gave such good, sound advice that Sydney felt completely at ease. As she watched Emily's and Sloane's eyes find each other throughout the night, there was no question why Sloane was so obviously in love with his wife.

I wonder why they never had children, she thought now as she entered the retinal scanning area. *Emily would have made a terrific mother.* Once the system verified her clearance, Sydney stepped through a set of doors into the bustling activity of SD-6.

Smiling at the agents she recognized, she walked past rows of silver-toned desks and flashing computer monitors to the conference room. Sloane had asked her to report here, and she was hoping that meant something good—namely, a new mission.

"Agent Bristow," Sloane said cordially, coming out from his office as she rounded the corner.

"Hi! Good morning," Sydney said, following him toward the large conference room called Optech. "I had such a great time last night. Your house is lovely, and Emily is—"

Although his expression remained pleasant, a tiny warning shadow flashed in Sloane's eyes. "Let's get to the business at hand, Agent Bristow," he said, cutting her off. Sydney didn't miss the repetition of "Agent Bristow." No more "Sydney, dear." *And definitely no more Arvin.*

For a moment, she felt hurt at the formal, distant way he had greeted her. *Don't be silly,* she scolded herself as they walked into the room. Of course that was how it had to be. Just because they had socialized together the night before didn't mean they were suddenly going to start high-fiving each other or exchanging SD-6 office gossip.

Instead of feeling hurt, Sydney should feel *privileged* that Sloane even included her in his personal life, she decided, straightening her shoulders.

"Agent Bristow." There at the long sleek table sat Noah Hicks. Instinctively Sydney smoothed back her perfect ponytail. Why did he always pop up when she least expected to see him?

"Agent Hicks," she replied, her tone businesslike. She'd take her cue from Sloane. Mixing your personal life with your professional one simply wasn't, well, professional. She took a seat at the table in the center of the room and checked the flat-screen monitor in front of her. A sphere-shaped screen saver bounced from corner to corner. She resisted the impulse to tap a key and instead looked expectantly at Sloane.

Her handler stood at the head of the room. He picked up a small black remote and clicked a button. A large retractable screen slid down from the ceiling.

"I have a project for you, Sydney. Something I hope you'll find helpful in your training."

Sydney's heart fluttered. "Of course. Great." She fought the urge to glance at Noah. Were they going to be sent off together again, like that trip to Paris? Maybe they'd be working in Spain. Or one of those picture-perfect Greek islands like—

"Votre francais, c'est bien?" Sloane asked suddenly.

Sydney didn't hesitate. *"Oui, bien sûr."*

Sloane smiled. "You're an excellent student of

languages, Sydney. In fact, you've excelled in each exercise and every mission you've had in your time with SD-6."

"Well, thank you," Sydney said, this time in English.

"But there's always room for more training. And this summer we have a special opportunity. I'm sending you to Ontario, Canada. You'll be joining four other newly trained agents for a weeklong instruction session."

"You mean I'm going to summer school?" Sydney blurted out before she could stop herself.

Noah chuckled.

Sloane rubbed his eyebrow with his thumb. "Not school, per se, Sydney. It's more of a refinement of the skills you've already mastered. Along with French language immersion classes, you'll spend a day at an intensive rock-climbing course and spend time with our colleagues across the border, trailing them on their customs and border protocol."

"Oh," Sydney said, deflating a bit. It sounded okay, but she'd been itching to get another assignment.

"And there's a mission for you as well," Sloane said, as if reading her mind. He clicked a button on his remote, and a black-and-white photograph of a middle-aged man flashed on the screen. "In the late 1950s there was a wildly brilliant government scientist named Carl Sanderling," Sloane explained. "Sanderling was fascinated by Niagara Falls—their power, their force, their sheer beauty—and this fascination became his downfall."

Sydney leaned forward, gazing into the face of the man in the photograph, searching for some indication that he was going to go over the edge, literally. But there was nothing except slightly unkempt hair, a thin nose, and large, expressionless eyes.

"He had traveled to Niagara Falls to attend a symposium on energy," Sloane continued, "but his real purpose was to further explore his interest by exchanging top-secret information with Russian agents on how to harness the power of the falls. Sanderling was a notorious record keeper, with pages of notes and photographs of models he had constructed in his possession. But Sanderling plunged to his death into the falls while at the symposium. His body washed ashore a few days later."

"Those barrels aren't what they're cracked up to be," Noah whispered to Sydney. She frowned at him. *Why is Noah here, anyway?* she wondered, her stomach flip-flopping with anxiety. *Is he going to*

Canada with me? It wasn't like he needed any training. . . . He had proven his capabilities as an ace agent time and again.

Sloane continued. "SD-6 has recently come into possession of Carl Sanderling's diary. We believe that his death was no accident—our intel suggests that he had learned that the Russian agents were not interested in the mere exchange of information but had a nefarious purpose to their quest. SD-6 believes that Sanderling hid his notes and photographs in a crevice in one of the tunnels behind the falls before plunging to his death." Sloane looked directly at Sydney. "SD-6 wants those notes."

"I'll get them," Sydney said confidently, feeling the now-familiar surge of pride that came with being given a new assignment to complete.

Sloane slid a black leather portfolio across the conference table. "Everything you'll need to know about Sanderling as well as a complete dossier on Niagara Falls topography is here. You'll leave L.A. on Wednesday."

Sydney nodded. "What will my alias be?"

"No alias." Small lines around Sloane's eyes crinkled as he smiled. "Everyone at the training seminar will know who you are."

"What about Agent Hicks?" Sydney asked, her

curiosity getting the better of her. "I mean, is he, um, coming too?" She casually glanced over at Noah. He winked back.

Infuriating!

"Agent Hicks is on his way to Hong Kong in one hour," Sloane said, giving no explanation of why Noah was in the room to begin with. "You are on your own, Agent Bristow."

"Think you can handle it?" Noah asked after Sloane gave a few more instructions, then walked out of the room. His eyes widened innocently as Sydney scowled at him.

"Gee, I think so," she retorted, tucking the portfolio carefully under her arm. Noah followed her into the hallway. She cleared her throat. "Don't you have a plane to catch or something?"

"French class," Noah mused, scratching his stubbled chin. "Well, all I can say is, *bon courage et bonne chance.*"

Of course Noah knew French. How could she forget the way he had surprised her when they were in Paris? She'd listened to him mutilate the language and had chalked him up as a hopeless tourist—only to gape in awe as he later rattled off the Romance language fluently. The horrible accent had merely been part of his cover. And her own lack of command over the language had been what prompted her to dive into her French studies this past semester as if her life depended on it.

Which perhaps it would someday.

"Oh, I'm sure you'll be learning all sorts of useful things," Noah went on, his eyes dancing. "*J'ai un grand désire de manger des escargots.* Or perhaps, *Elle ne dort qu'avec des tranquillisants.* Or, no, I've got it, *Tu penses à un ancien amour: auquel penses-tu?*" he suggested with another aggravating wink.

"*Jamais.*" Sydney sniffed. "Whatever it is we study, I'm not concerned. French is one of my better classes. Now if you'll excuse me, I've got some packing to do." She turned on her heel and strode down the hallway, ignoring the sound of Noah's chuckle.

Except she couldn't ignore him completely. His last words, *Tu penses à un ancien amour: auquel penses-tu?,* played over and over in her head.

Noah Hicks wasn't as smart as he thought he was.

Because how could I think of an old love when he is very much my present one?

4

"BRISTOW? SYDNEY BRISTOW?" ASKED the gray-haired man, holding up a small white card. Sydney's last name was printed neatly in capital letters below the car service's logo. The man was waiting in the Buffalo International Airport's baggage claim area.

"That's me," Sydney said, smiling. It felt strange to hear her real name being used on a mission; she'd been so many people since joining SD-6, from Kate Jones to Carrie Wainwright to Adriana Nichita, it was hard to keep her aliases straight. She was sure she'd get used to it. *Someday.*

"My name is Ben and the car's out front," he said, gesturing to the sliding glass doors. "Want to grab your bags?"

She pulled out the handle on her tote and slung her black leather purse over her shoulder. "I didn't check any luggage, so I'm ready to go."

Moments later she was settled comfortably into the back leather seat of a black Lincoln town car. She stared out the window as they pulled out of the parking lot at the airport and merged into the late-afternoon traffic. She'd left L.A. at seven a.m., but with changing planes in Chicago and the three-hour time difference, it was already after four in the afternoon.

Sydney remembered seeing Buffalo on TV in her childhood, wild scenes of sky-high piles of snow and excited kids getting to stay home from school. The idea of having a snow day, an unexpected day home from school, had always seemed like so much fun. *But it wasn't like I would have had anyone to spend it with,* Sydney thought. Today, there wasn't a snowflake in sight. In fact, Sydney noted as they merged onto another highway and Ben cut someone off, things didn't look much different than they did in any of the cities she'd visited.

Well, maybe except for Paris, she thought wistfully.

That trip had been the highlight of her time in SD-6, she had decided. Besides the amazing beauty of the city, with all its garrets and spires and the Seine wending its way past cozy cafes and pricey boutiques (not that she'd had any time to spend in either), and the romance she'd kindled with Noah (or at least, she thought she had kindled one), what had been so nice was that for once she'd felt as if she had a confidante. Noah Hicks was someone who knew her real identity. He knew that she worked for SD-6 and it was okay that he knew. Being able to be out in the open about that part of her life had been such a relief.

This training opportunity was a chance to make friends too, in a way. Sydney hadn't met any other trainees during her time at SD-6; instead, all she saw were highly efficient agents who had lots more experience than she did. Sydney supposed that was a good thing—after all, the fact that she was included in this group meant that her superiors had a great deal of faith in her.

"Enjoy yourself, Sydney," Sloane had told her when she had called to check in earlier that day. "This is a rare opportunity for you to meet some people who are in a similar situation to yours."

If such a person really exists, I'd love to meet her! she thought, closing her eyes. *Yes, any girl geniuses raised in a one-parent household by a father who barely spent a moment with her and who were recruited by the CIA during their freshman year of college, step up to the plate!*

She must have drifted off, because it only seemed like a few minutes later that she was woken up. "Ms. Bristow? We'll be crossing the Peace Bridge in a moment," Ben spoke up from the front. He was guiding the town car into one of several lanes feeding into the bridge traffic.

Sydney blinked. They were already at the Canadian border. She opened her purse and pulled out her real passport. Flipping through it, she realized that she didn't have any stamps. No blurred foreign words with exotic place names, no evidence that she'd ever even been out of the country. All she had were her memories.

The car pulled up to a window and tilted slightly to the right so that the customs officer could get a clear look inside. Ben slid his window down and Sydney did the same.

"Country of citizenship?" asked a young Canadian customs officer.

"U.S.," Ben said.

"U.S.," Sydney echoed.

"Where are you going?" the officer asked Sydney.

"Niagara Falls," Sydney said, giving him a smile.

"Purpose?"

"I'm meeting some friends and we're going rock climbing." While it was fine for Sydney to use her real name, Sloane had advised her not to give any details of her mission to the customs officers. It would slow things down. Once she was with her fellow agents, they'd be back at the border crossing soon enough.

"How long are you staying?"

"Just a few days," Sydney told him.

The officer glanced at Ben's driver's license, then handed it back.

"Don't fall," he said, waving them through.

Sydney stuck her passport back in her purse. The officer hadn't even looked at it. *Well, I'm sure glad I didn't come up with an elaborate disguise for that,* she thought, glancing down at her black cotton shorts and her most comfortable sandals.

It was going to be nice being able to be Sydney Bristow on a mission. Being a student was something she could do pretty well.

But as for being herself? That was something she kept practicing every day.

* * *

"Thank you!" Sydney called over her shoulder as Ben pulled away from the entrance to the Maple Leaf Lodge. The large building in front of her was the guest registration entrance, and one-story wings sprawled out on either side. She had been slightly disappointed to see that the accommodations were several blocks from the falls. *You aren't here to be a tourist,* she reminded herself as she strode into the lobby and squinted, her eyes adjusting to the light. Comfortable couches and rustic chairs filled the generously sized lobby, and a gigantic chandelier made from moose antlers hung overhead. In fact, she noted as she took in her surroundings, there were actual stuffed animal heads lining the walls. *Nice.*

"I'm checking in," she told the man behind the desk. "I'm with the rock-climbing group led by Tad Sinclair? Sydney Bristow."

"Oh, yes." He typed something into a computer, then handed Sydney a crisp white packet and an electronic key card. "Your room is in the west wing," he said, pointing discreetly to the number 357 on her card key. "The other members of your party have already checked in. They're meeting in the Whirlpool Lounge." He cocked his head to her left.

"Oh," Sydney said, looking down at her wrinkled clothes. She had been hoping to take a quick shower and change before meeting her fellow agents, but she didn't want to miss anything important.

"I can have a bellhop take your things to your room if you want," the man offered, gesturing to a young guy with messy black hair. He wore a drab brown uniform and was leaning against the wall, smoking a cigarette.

The Maple Leaf Lodge has a bellhop? And he's it? Sydney hesitated. Then her practical side took over. She nodded and picked up the packet, forcing herself not to look over at Slacker Bellhop. "Okay, thanks."

Inside the Whirlpool Lounge five pairs of eyes turned to look at her when she walked in. Five people were standing around a large conference table that was covered with cans of soda, bottled water, and several bowls of snack food.

"Hi!" she said to no one in particular, feeling a blush come into her cheeks. No matter how much training she had, no one ever seemed to be able to tell her how to refrain from turning red whenever she was embarrassed. "I'm—"

"Agent Bristow," finished an older man, his dark brown hair cropped short, his clothes casual but professional. He smiled at her. "I'm Agent Henry. And that clown over there"—he pointed to a burly man in a blue polo shirt who was stuffing a handful of potato chips in his mouth—"is Agent Sinclair."

"I'm glad to be here," Sydney said, shaking their hands. "Sorry I'm late."

"You aren't. We were just getting to know each other a little," Agent Henry said.

A tall guy with sandy blond hair, a slim build, and an easy smile walked over. "Would you like a Coke?" he asked, cracking open a fresh can. He looked about her age.

"That would be great," Sydney said, happily taking it from him.

"I'm Paul Riley. I work at SD-2 in Chicago."

"Maureen Paladino," piped up a young woman with short dark hair, a bottle of water in her hand.

"The Midwest?" Sydney guessed after hearing her speak.

Maureen laughed. "St. Louis. SD-15. And you've got to be from California."

"But I don't have an accent and I'm not blond *or* tan," Sydney protested with a laugh.

"But you do have an LAX sticker on your purse," pointed out a short, muscular African American guy. He stuck out his hand. "Greg Williams. SD-3 in New York."

"Nice to meet all of you," Sydney said, a feeling of genuine warmth bubbling up inside her. It felt so good to finally meet people like herself, bright, devoted young people who were dedicating their lives to defending their country. She wasn't entirely alone after all.

"Hey! Hi!" A striking young woman with long blond hair and huge blue eyes hurried into the room clutching a small orange foil bag. "Leave it to me to step out to go grab a bag of potato chips and miss meeting my roomie."

"Me?" Sydney said, surprised. She hadn't counted on having a roommate. The girl looked slightly older than Sydney, and she was beautiful, with a heart-shaped face and delicate features. But Sydney didn't get any prima donna vibes—instead, she had an immediate gut feeling that they were going to be friends.

Agent Henry perched himself on top of the table. "Sharing rooms cuts down our costs and helps build bonds between agents. Harling and Bristow, Riley and Williams, and Paladino, you drew the lucky straw—a single."

"Having a roommate makes sense," Sydney said, turning her gaze back to the girl. Maybe Sloane was right. Maybe she would make a new friend here.

The girl gave Sydney a warm smile as she introduced herself. "I'm Stephanie Harling, from SD-2."

"So you two came here together?" Sydney asked, looking over at Paul. That would be kind of nice, having another agent to train with. *Especially one as cute as Paul.* Then Sydney's mind flickered to Noah. *And especially one who's on the same level.*

"Yep," Stephanie said, dropping into a chair. Her hair fanned over her slightly freckled shoulders. "I don't know how the folks back home are going to get along without us."

Sydney thought of her own "folks back home." They consisted of one person: Francie.

Agent Sinclair rapped his knuckles on the table. "Okay, agents. Five more minutes of chitchat, and then I'm going to go over the agenda for our days here in Niagara Falls. I'm sure you'll find them exhausting, exhilarating, and hell, maybe a bit exasperating."

"Sounds like my last girlfriend," Greg muttered beside Sydney.

As the other agents laughed and picked at the remaining snacks, Sydney excused herself and went out into the lobby.

Time to give the folks back home a call.

*　*　*

"This is ten times harder than being a waitress!" Francie complained, her voice clear as a whistle even though she was thousands of miles away in New Mexico. "I'm like the Parkers' new personal servant. 'Francie, I need a juice box.' 'Francie, I'm hot.' 'Francie, I'm bored.'" A large whoosh of air came over the phone. "Kids are totally spoiled these days!"

Sydney laughed, leaning back into the lumpy lobby couch and cradling the phone under her chin. "Remember what you said. It's the experience that counts. After all, you could be here with me"— she hesitated, hating the lie that was about to come out of her mouth— "in good old smog-filled L.A."

Francie snorted. "Like you'd ever go out and enjoy the day anyway. Don't you have the bank's logo tattooed on your butt by now?"

"Actually it's on my stomach."

Sydney knew she couldn't really blame Francie for feeling the way she did, but sometimes she didn't want to hear it. And this was one of those times.

There was a moment of silence. "I'm sorry, Syd. Don't be mad," Francie said, her voice sounding tired and small. "I guess I just feel kind of lonesome today. And like maybe I made the wrong decision taking this job." She sighed. "I'm here in this huge house trying to make three different kinds of tacos for three wild, sweaty kids while Mr. and Mrs. Parker eat lunch at some chichi local restaurant. But I shouldn't complain to you. You're probably driving to the bank right now."

"I'm not working today," Sydney blurted out. "I'm—I'm going to just, uh, hang out."

"Are you kidding me? I'm away and suddenly you're going to just 'hang out'? Jeez! Are you going to the beach?"

"Um—"

"No, wait," Francie cut her off. "Tell me you're not going shopping at the Beverly Center. Or worse, the Farmer's Market. Are you? I am *dying* for an empanada from Benny's!"

Sydney looked up at the giant stuffed bear head hanging over the Maple Leaf Lodge's check-in desk.

Then she let out a sigh. "Me too."

* * *

Sydney took out a khaki skirt from her suitcase and frowned, her forehead crinkling. "This was supposed to be wrinkle free," she said, giving it a frustrated shake and then hanging it up in the hotel room closet.

"I have an iron if you need one," Stephanie

called over to her. She was kneeling in front of the TV, running her hands under the set and over the back. "It's clean." Then, as Sydney tossed a few pairs of shorts into a drawer, Stephanie moved over to the telephone, pulled out a miniature tool kit from her duffel bag, and began to take the receiver apart.

Sydney's new roommate was unbelievably thorough. After quickly unpacking her belongings, she had tested the door's locks, scanned the room for bugs, checked the window seals and the air-conditioning unit, and had ended up on her hands and knees in front of the TV. *Maybe I've been a little too negligent,* Sydney thought worriedly. "Do you always do this when you stay at a hotel?" she asked, curious.

Stephanie shrugged. "You can't be too safe," she said, peering into the coat closet.

Sydney followed her gaze. Nothing but old wire hangers and a few musty cobwebs. "How long have you been with SD-2?" Sydney asked, zipping up her now empty suitcase and tossing it onto the luggage rack.

"Sixteen months," Stephanie said. "I was recruited during my senior year at the University of Chicago. It sure added some excitement to my dual major of political science and Japanese."

"So you're through with school?" Sydney asked enviously. It wasn't that she wanted to wish away her college years . . . but it was hard to concentrate in her foreign cultures class when she was actually experiencing the very things she was reading about. And coming up with creative stories for her classmates on why she was absent so often was not an easy task.

"I graduated last June." Stephanie pumped her fist. "Woo-hoo! No more all-nighters! Of course, it was a little anticlimactic watching all my friends hunt for jobs and be wooed by Fortune 500 companies while I pretended to be psyched to get a permanent offer from the"—she made air quotes—"'insurance company' I've been working at."

"Oh, wow." Sydney hadn't thought that far ahead, but she could imagine it now. *The stuff is going to hit the fan if I tell Francie I'm going to work for Credit Dauphine full-time!* She sighed. She'd cross that bridge when she came to it.

"I've got three years left at UCLA," Sydney said, half to herself. "Then I guess I'll work for SD-6 full-time." After all she had been through in the past year, Sydney knew she would be putting aside her plan to become an English teacher, like her mother had, and committing to a life of service to her country. But somehow the thought of working somewhere for the rest of her life—even the CIA—was a little daunting. She couldn't let herself think too much about life after college. *I still have to pass my sophomore honors history class next semester, and Professor Elgin is supposed to be a holy terror!*

Feeling slightly guilty as she watched Stephanie continue her thorough room sweep, Sydney got down on the carpet and halfheartedly looked under the beds for anything suspect. Ugh. Nothing but some serious dust bunnies and an old deodorant bottle. She sat up, brushing her hands off on her shorts.

I wonder if Stephanie's on a mission too, Sydney thought, watching as the other agent crouched down and felt the closet floor. Would it be wrong to ask her? It could be kind of fun to compare the gadgets they had. In the zippered interior compartment of her suitcase were several new state-of-the-art devices Graham had concocted for her: a digital camera built into the palm of a fashionable leather glove; a lightweight bulletproof water poncho, a tube of lipstick that contained a sedative, and her favorite, a waterproof wristwatch that emitted a laser that immobilized someone for up to sixty seconds, similar to the effects of a stun gun. "Where were you when I was being hit on by all those drunken frat boys last fall?" she had joked when Graham had shown her how the gadgets worked.

"Well, what do you know," Stephanie said suddenly, startling Sydney out of her thoughts. Slowly, the blond agent peeled off a small black disk that was affixed to the back of the luggage rack. "Looks like someone didn't want to miss a word of our conversation."

To: sydney.bristow@credit-dauphine.com

From: noah.hicks@credit-dauphine.com

Subject: apparel

~~Dear Agent Bristow,~~
~~Dear Sydney,~~
Sydney,
Just wondering what size kimono you wear.
~~Love,~~
~~Wish you were here,~~
~~Love,~~
~~The guy who drives you crazy and you love it~~
~~Agent Hicks~~
See ya,
Noah

To: noah.hicks@creditdauphine.com

From: sydney.bristow@credit-dauphine.com

Subject: Out of Office AutoReply: apparel

Hello. You have reached the office of Sydney Bristow at Credit Dauphine. I will be working on the filing system in the main bank branch this week and will be checking my e-mail only periodically. I will respond to your e-mail as soon as possible.

5

SYDNEY SMILED AT THE other agents and made
polite small talk when they met at the hotel restaurant for dinner later that night, but she was grateful
when the waiter handed her an oversized plastic-
covered menu that she could duck behind. She
didn't want anyone to be able to read what was on
her face.

SD agents were supposed to be able to conceal
their emotions, but Sydney found that hard to do,
especially when her heart was racing and her mind
was darting every which way.

She and Stephanie had decided it was best not

to say anything about the bug to the others just yet. At this point, there was nothing anyone could do. But even though Sydney wasn't talking about it, she couldn't stop thinking about it. Who could have tapped their room? And why? The mission she was working on for Sloane was old news. Nobody would be interested in Sanderling's research now. Would they?

"So what are you having?" Paul asked from the seat beside her.

"Um, I think the steak," Sydney said, hoping that it was actually a choice on the menu. The only reason she could think of for someone to spy on their room was if they were trying to get to Stephanie. And the only reason someone would try to get to Stephanie was if she was on a mission.

And if she is, I'm going to find out what it is.

* * *

"No freaking way. They sent you to ammunitions training in your first month?" Maureen put down her fork in protest. "That is so not fair. I had to wait until my third!"

Greg took another bite of his sauce-covered pork chop. "Where was your first mission?"

"Detroit," Maureen said slowly. "Where was yours?"

Greg shrugged. "Nowhere great." He paused. "Bali."

Paul high-fived him. "Me too, dude!"

Sydney laughed into her cloth napkin as Maureen gave Greg and Paul each a mock punch. Dinner had turned out to be surprisingly good, both in food and in company. Once their meals had come and she had begun to eat, Sydney was able to forget, at least for a little while, about the black disk Stephanie had located. And it was fun to share anecdotes with people who were just like her. People who could completely understand the life she was leading because they were leading it too.

"How about you, Sydney? Where did you go on your first mission? Paris?" Maureen asked sarcastically, nibbling at a piece of bread.

"No . . . they saved that for my second one," she deadpanned as Greg and Paul howled with laughter. "My first was right in L.A. At a rock concert."

"Who was playing?" Stephanie asked, her blue eyes wide. "Don't tell me you had to escort some gorgeous guitar god to his dressing room."

Sydney shook her head. "No, nothing like that." Everyone at the table worked for a division of SD, but she wasn't sure what she should reveal and what she should keep quiet. In any case, the memory of that first mission—one she didn't even know she was being sent on—was one she wanted to forget.

A spoon clinking on a wineglass got her attention. "Okay, everyone. I hope you enjoyed your dinner tonight," Agent Henry said as he stood. "We've held this retreat at the Maple Leaf Lodge for the past five years, and I can tell you that the lemon meringue pie is something to behold."

"Looks like you made the right choice, then," Sydney whispered to her roommate as a waitress carried in a tray of desserts and deposited a large slice of pie in front of Stephanie. "I can never resist ice cream. It's my weakness."

Then she grew quiet as she watched Agent Henry's eyes travel from person to person, taking in every detail. She hadn't quite figured him out yet. "I've got a special offer for you tonight," Agent Henry announced, waving a business-sized envelope in front of them. Okay, she definitely didn't have him figured out. "I've got a gift certificate for dinner for two at the best restaurant in Niagara Falls for the first person to turn in a wiretap or bugging device."

Sydney blinked as Stephanie, a puzzled look on

her face, stood up, removed the small black disk from her pants pocket, and deposited it in Agent Henry's outstretched palm. To her surprise, Greg got up too—and seconds later gave an identical bug to a grinning Agent Sinclair.

Nervous laughter spread throughout the room, and then Sydney felt her face flushing that familiar shade of pink. *We weren't being spied on,* she thought, realizing what had happened. *The bugs were part of our training!*

Stephanie gave her a sheepish look. "I am such a dork," she whispered back.

Relief washed over Sydney. No one was spying on them. No one was after Sanderling. *But what was the purpose of putting bugs in our room?* she wondered. A glance at the superior agents in the room told her she was about to find out.

"All right, we're ready for you," Agent Sinclair called into the hallway, motioning to someone out of viewing range. The young agents craned their necks as several members of the hotel staff paraded into the room.

"Agents, I'd like you to meet . . . your fellow agents."

A collective gasp went out from the group as a woman Sydney had seen dressed as a maid earlier stepped forward. She was now wearing a sleek black pantsuit and a pearl choker that would cost a domestic worker's yearly salary. "Good evening, everyone. I'm Agent Mary Cunningham." She turned to Greg. "You were so accommodating, Agent Williams. Not only did you leave the door open when I brought the extra towels you had delivered, you kindly took a shower, giving me ample time to search through all of your belongings." She winked. "Love the silk boxers."

Greg swore under his breath, then held his hands up in mock surrender. "Guilty as charged."

Sydney couldn't believe who was next in line— Slacker Bellboy! His hair was still long and messy, but he had crisp khakis and a button-down shirt for a uniform now. "Hey, all. I'm Agent Monrovi." He walked over to her and took a thin silver chain out of his pocket. "I think this belongs to you, Agent Bristow."

"My necklace!" Sydney's fingers closed around the delicate piece of jewelry. It had belonged to her mother, and she kept it in a small box tucked away in her cosmetics bag. She hadn't even noticed it was missing.

And the humiliation went on. A room service waiter had Maureen's Palm Pilot. Paul had failed to notice the tiny camera installed above his bathroom sink.

"Glad to know you floss!" Agent Sinclair told him as everyone chuckled sheepishly.

And Sydney was further horrified to learn that her entire cell phone conversation with Francie was noted word for word by a "hotel receptionist." "Too bad you're stuck in smoggy L.A.," the agent who had sat behind the desk said with a slight smirk. Sydney wanted to slap her.

"What about Stephanie?" Maureen asked impulsively. "You must have something on her."

Paul reached over and patted Stephanie on the shoulder. "You don't know Steph, Maureen. The girl is flawless."

Stephanie smiled a slightly embarrassed smile. "Paul is right," Agent Henry spoke up. "Stephanie is the only agent in this room who came through with a perfect score. Not only did she not let herself get compromised by anyone on the hotel staff, she made sure to do a thorough sweep of her room and discover the bug we had planted earlier."

"Everyone had a bug in their room," Agent Sinclair told them as the formerly disguised agents said their good-byes and exited, "so Maureen, your homework for tonight is to go back and find yours."

The young woman nodded curtly. "Will do."

Agent Henry walked over and handed Stephanie the gift certificate envelope. "And I want everyone in this room to give some serious thought to what went on here tonight. One perfect score is pathetic. There are five agents in this room. How many perfect scores should we have, Agent Bristow?"

"Five, sir," she replied.

"This should be old hat to you by now," Agent Henry went on. "*Always* check your room—for bugs, for taps, for God knows what. *Never* let anyone carry your luggage, and *never* let your luggage out of your sight."

"You know, like those taped warnings that play over and over again at the airport," Greg joked.

But Sydney knew it wasn't a joke. It was a silly, stupid mistake—and seeing a guy she'd written off as Slacker Bellhop dangle her precious silver necklace in front of her eyes had proved it. Stephanie hadn't been too cautious—she was doing her job, the job Sydney should be doing on a regular, consistent basis.

Sydney stared down at the small glass bowl that a waitress had put in front of her several minutes before. What had once been coffee ice cream was now a brown puddle. Ice cream had a way of doing that when you weren't looking.

Sydney wouldn't get caught not looking again.

"I have to tell you, I was kind of disappointed in the bathtub," Stephanie said as she splashed warm water on her face and then patted it dry with a towel. "When I found out we were coming to Niagara Falls, honeymoon central . . ."

"I know! I was thinking they were going to have a cheesy heart-shaped one," Sydney confessed, putting her toothbrush back in its holder. She looked into the large beveled mirror that hung over the double vanity and wiped a dab of toothpaste from her lip. She was glad she had her bathrobe—the air conditioner was stuck on HIGH COOL and the motel room was freezing. *I'll probably have icicles on my eyelashes when I wake up tomorrow.*

"The funniest thing ever was I had to stay in this total dive once, and the room had a vibrating bed." Stephanie giggled. "You had to pay fifty cents to get it to move!"

"Eww!" Sydney wrinkled her nose and walked over to her double bed. She sat down and gave the mattress a firm thump. "I'll take a standard box spring any day."

Stephanie plopped down on her own bed, which let out a loud creak. "Me too."

Sydney bit her lip. "You know, I feel really bad that you got stuck with that lumpy thing."

Stephanie waved her guilt away. "No problem. I'm so tired tonight I could sleep on a rock."

"You'll have the chance to do that tomorrow," Sydney reminded her. They were going to a rock-climbing class early in the morning.

Stephanie nodded. "Yeah." She reached over to the nightstand and grabbed the bottle of Neutrogena moisturizer that sat there and poured some on her long tan legs. "You know, sometimes I can't believe the stuff I'm doing now that I'm part of SD-2. I mean, rock climbing? That's something people on *Road Rules* do, not me."

Sydney had often felt the same way. Chasing after rock stars who were arms dealers, being sent to some remote Scottish island posing as a Romanian heiress . . . sometimes she couldn't believe the life she was leading was actually hers. "I know exactly how you feel. Do you . . . do you ever have any regrets? About what we do?"

Her roommate hesitated, then shook her head. "Not really. Only that I wish I could tell my mom about this crazy life."

Sydney smiled ruefully. "It's so hard keeping things a secret. I hate it sometimes."

Stephanie stared down at her chipped red toenail polish, then back over at Sydney. "Me too. But I'm not keeping it a secret from my mom. She died when I was twelve. Leukemia."

"Really?" Sydney blurted out. "My mother died when I was six. In a car accident."

"I'm so sorry," Stephanie said, her eyes full of empathy. Neither of them said anything for several minutes. Then Stephanie sighed. "I didn't know how to deal with it and I was twelve. I can't imagine having that happen to you when you're six. Are you and your dad close?"

Sydney choked back a bitter laugh. "Close isn't the word. Strangers? Enemies? Now that's more like it."

"My dad and I don't see each other much," Stephanie confessed. She went on to tell Sydney that he worked in business development for a major computer manufacturer and that he was a total workaholic. "I wasn't even sure he was going to show up for my high school graduation," she said, flopping down on her mattress. *Creak.*

Could we be any more alike? Sydney thought, staring at her new friend in amazement. *Our moms are dead, our fathers are fanatical about their jobs, and we both happen to be college students who were recruited to work for the CIA.*

Then Stephanie hopped off the bed and rummaged

around in her dresser drawer, finally holding up a pair of red cable-knit socks. "I have two pairs of these, and I swear they keep your feet totally warm."

Okay, that seals it. "You rock!" Sydney said, happily taking the pair Stephanie held out to her. "My feet always freeze at night and I forgot sleep socks."

Stephanie clicked off the overhead lights and picked up the television remote. "Did you want to watch anything? We could get a movie."

Sydney shook her head and put on the socks. "Nah. Actually I'm really enjoying talking to you." She stood up and pulled down the bedspread, then shot an apologetic look over at Stephanie. "It's so nice to talk to someone and not feel like I'm keeping this big secret from them. I have this great roommate back at UCLA, Francie, who's actually my very best friend at school, and I have to lie to her all the time." She wondered what Francie was doing now. *Probably creating a Georgia O'Keeffe–inspired finger-paint masterpiece.* "She thinks I work for a bank and is always giving me grief for ditching her for my job."

Stephanie hooted. "Multiply that times two! Ingrid and Emma were my roommates at the University of Chicago. They're the ones who got these swanky finance jobs, and they think I settled to work at the insurance company. And they are constantly bombarding me with invitations to go shopping, go to parties, go to the Art Institute, you name it."

"Two roommates?" Sydney gave a shudder, partly for effect and partly because she was freezing. "I definitely couldn't deal with that. Lying to one person is hard enough. It's so frustrating having her think badly of me, when if she only knew what I was really doing . . ." Sydney trailed off, imagining how Francie would react if she found out Sydney worked for the CIA. *You're a spy? Yeah, right. And I'm Julia Roberts.*

"I'm always paranoid that they're going to show up at the Peerless Insurance Company unannounced and ask to see me, and I'll be off working somewhere."

"Are you working now?" Sydney said before she could catch herself. "I mean, during this training . . . do you, uh, have a mission?" *Dumb, dumb, dumb,* Sydney scolded herself as she watched Stephanie's face tense up. If she had learned anything in the past few hours, it was that she and Stephanie had a lot in common.

And if her new friend was anything like Sydney, she wouldn't feel exactly comfortable talking about something as private and personal as her life in the CIA.

"Forget I asked," Sydney said hastily, wishing

she could take the question back. "It's really none of my business." Despite her near-perfect comfort level with her new friend, it wasn't as if *she* was going to suddenly start spilling details about Sanderling and Sloane. That just wasn't protocol, friend or not.

Stephanie shook her head. "No, don't be silly." She giggled. "And to answer your question, other than to practice my horrible French, no. I don't have a mission." Then she let out a monster-sized yawn. "I'm sorry, Sydney. I'm so beat. Can we talk more tomorrow?"

"Sure," Sydney said, clicking off the reading light above her head and snuggling down under the covers.

That is, if I'm not frozen solid by then.

6

"THAT'S IT, SYDNEY. KEEP your focus."

That was easy for her instructor to say, Sydney thought as she looked warily up at the rocky cliffside in front of her where the rock-climbing guide, Chris, stood along with the other members of Sydney's group. After spending the morning going over the basics like tying knots, getting into harnesses, and belaying at an Ontario rock-climbing gym, Sydney and her fellow agents were now undergoing a day of rappelling instruction on a cliffside not far from downtown Toronto.

"We're on real rock, baby!" Greg had said when they arrived.

"Show us the ropes," Paul had added, carrying his heavy gear as if it was light as a crepe. "Those indoor gyms are for sissies. This is for the big boys."

"Don't even get me started," Maureen had shot back, waving a friction boot at him.

The gorgeous scenery had awed Sydney, boulders jutting out against a picture-perfect blue sky. Now, though, the scenery took a backseat to the task at hand.

Sydney had been trained in the basics of the sport, as had everyone else when they had been recruited. The course they were taking was meant to enhance their skills—and to be a bonding experience.

And if I stay in this location any longer, I'm going to bond with a large gray spider, Sydney thought as the thing idled inches from her face. With a deep, steadying breath, she considered her options, then moved her right foot carefully to the next safe resting place, the rock underneath her hands rough and warm.

"Get the lead out, Bristow!" Chris shouted. "We can't wait all day. You all have to move or we'll never fit everything in."

"Come on, Syd. You're almost there," Stephanie's

voice called out encouragingly from the ledge above her.

And her roommate was right. Sydney only had two more moves to complete. Seconds later she was on top of the cliff.

Paul gave her a high five as she turned around and looked at the spectacular view behind her. "Way to challenge the vertical."

"Thanks," she said breathlessly, looking back over her shoulder at where she had just climbed. Now that she had reached the top, her on-edge nerves were gone. Instead excitement churned adrenaline through her bloodstream. "Bring on the next cliff," she called over to Chris.

He laughed. "Oh, I will."

After lunch, Chris led the group along a dusty trail to an even more breathtaking cliff. This one was so high, Sydney couldn't see the summit.

"Piece of cake," Greg scoffed as they took it in.

Sydney wasn't so sure about that. "It looks pretty difficult," she said to Stephanie. Her roommate had been the clear star of that day's climbing expedition, at times seeming to know more than their instructor did.

Stephanie shook her head. "You can't approach a climb like that. You need to walk up to this cliff, tell it you are about to kick its butt, and then do it."

Sydney laughed. "Let me know if you're free the next time I have to go meet a stranger in a dark alley, okay?"

"Stephanie, Paul, you're on," Chris called, waving them over. They would be climbing in pairs. "This time we're going to see how you are with lead climbing. I normally would avoid doing this in combination with a regular climbing class, but you lot are, well, a special group."

Sydney wasn't sure what Agents Henry and Sinclair had told their young, muscular guide about their identity. For all she knew, he was an SD agent himself. "If this goes well, we'll be back for your high-angle rescue and evacuation course," Agent Henry told Chris as he and Agent Sinclair moseyed off for a cigarette break.

"What exactly does going well mean?" Sydney wondered out loud as she, Maureen, and Greg gathered on the side.

"It means SD-6 doesn't lose their yearlong investment," Greg said straightforwardly, and Sydney paused to think that, as crass as it sounded, it was probably the truth. Training an SD-6 agent had to cost the government a fortune—not to mention all the expenses that were accrued on various missions. Losing a trainee was certainly not on the government's agenda.

If my father only knew where his tax dollars were going! Sydney thought with a wry smile as she gazed around the sunny precipice.

As Stephanie and Paul set up their gear, the rest of the group listened as Chris explained how the climb would work.

"Capisce?" Chris said waggishly. Maureen gave him a thumbs-up. "See, you guys aren't the only ones who know a foreign language around here."

The climb was seconds away from beginning when Stephanie frantically motioned Sydney over. "Sydney, I feel like an idiot, but I really have to go to the bathroom," she whispered as Paul waited patiently nearby. "I mean, I need to get behind a boulder *now*."

"And you're telling me that because—"

"Because you heard Chris earlier," Stephanie whispered, quickly unhooking her harness. "He's been watching the clock all day. A bathroom break at 3:05 is not on his itinerary. Just take my place."

"But—" Sydney began apprehensively, glancing over at Paul and then up at the cliff. "I'm not ready!"

"Sure you are," Stephanie insisted, slipping out of her harness. "You've been the star climber all day long."

"Me?" Sydney protested. "But—"

"What's going on?" Paul said as he caught on to what was happening. A frown crossed his lips. "Steph, you can't just switch partners in the middle of a climb!"

"Well, I can and I did," Stephanie said, handing her gear to a disconcerted Sydney. "And it's not the middle of a climb. It hasn't even started. I'll be back before you guys are halfway up." She squeezed Sydney's hand. "Kick butt!"

Chris strode over. "I don't care who Paul has for a partner, but I do care that he *has* a partner. Let's move."

Swallowing her protest at this unorthodox change of plans, Sydney strapped herself into her harness, made sure that everything was in place, and followed Chris's instructions as she and Paul readied for their climb.

"I saw this documentary about climbers who climb choreographed to music," Paul said as they carefully began their ascent. "Rocks, bridges, skyscrapers—the world is their stage."

"Don't get any ideas," Sydney said as she climbed. They moved higher and higher up the incline, and soon the other agents were a good sixty feet below them.

She had slipped into a comfortable rhythm, her

foot and hand placement matching the composition of the mountain, anticipating Paul's every move as they ascended. Then the unthinkable happened. As Sydney went to place her foot in what she thought would be a secure hold, she slipped, showering rivulets of gravel on the group below.

As she fell back, she held her breath, waiting for the harness safety mechanism to take over.

But it didn't. Instead, she skidded down the side of the mountain, boulders bruising her shins, rock rubbing her hands raw.

This isn't supposed to happen, she thought, panicking, as Greg's words about SD-6 losing their investment flashed into her brain.

"Sydney!" Paul cried from above.

Sydney let out a strangled screech, scrambling wildly for something, anything, to hold on to. By a small miracle, she managed to clutch an exposed tree root. Her bare legs swung in the air, banging hard against the rock, and her heart was thumping out of control. "What's wrong with Bristow's harness?" she heard someone scream from below.

It seemed like hours that Sydney clasped the root before Paul navigated the cliff and helped her slowly climb back down.

"What the hell happened up there?" Greg demanded as Agent Sinclair went to help Paul with his harness and the rest of the group gathered around her. "You scared the crap out of us!"

"Out of you?" Sydney took a gulp of air. "One minute I felt secure and the next I was falling through thin air," she said, her legs wobbly on solid ground. She put her hands on her thighs and bent over, trying to regulate her breathing. The rush of blood and fear combined with the bright sun overhead had made her feel nauseous.

"If I were you, I'd give him hell," Maureen said as Paul made his way down and over to them. "Milk it for all it's worth."

Stephanie blinked back tears as Paul went right to her and gave her a hug. "I can't believe this," she choked out, squeezing her hands into fists. "It's my fault."

Paul brushed a lock of hair from Stephanie's face. "It's not anybody's fault," he said firmly, gazing into her eyes. His behavior was professional and consoling, but Sydney got the feeling from his body language that something else lay below the surface. Was something going on between Stephanie and Paul?

She tried to smile as Paul let go of Stephanie and came over and gave her a pat on the shoulder.

A hug for Stephanie, who was on solid ground,

and a pat for me, who dangled in midair. Okay, what's wrong with this picture?

"Man, Sydney, you really had me scared up there," he said, pulling back and shaking his head.

"Ditto," she said shakily. "Good thing I'm not going dancing tonight." Her legs were covered with bruises and bits of blood.

Paul smacked his forehead with his palm. "What am I standing here talking to you for? Let me go get the first-aid kit," he said. "That's the least I can do." As he jogged off, Stephanie wiped away a tear.

"That could have been me up there," Stephanie whispered so only Sydney could hear, her face drained of color. More tears slid down her white cheeks. "It *should* have been me. Someone did something to the equipment. Someone wanted this to happen."

"Don't be stupid. It was just an accident," Sydney insisted, wondering what she meant. "Just my dumb luck that it was me."

"And your dumb luck that saved you," Greg told Stephanie.

His words made Sydney pause.

Maybe dumb luck wasn't what had saved Stephanie. What had seemed an ill-timed moment for Stephanie to take a bathroom break had almost cost Sydney her life.

And she's more than a little upset about it. Her friend seemed almost guilty.

As if she had known something like this would happen all along.

*   *   *

After a shower to soothe her aching muscles, and then pizza and shop talk with Agents Henry and Sinclair and her fellow trainees later that night, Sydney begged off the game of Monopoly Greg was setting up in the hotel lobby. "I'm going to go for a run," she told him, gesturing to her blue nylon shorts she'd pulled on over an old pair of gray leggings and her red T-shirt covered with a nylon outer shirt in case it got cold.

"Do you think you're up to it?" he asked, eyeing her legs. "You took quite a beating today."

"In a day or so, I'll be as good as new," Sydney said.

Maureen stopped organizing the little piles of paper money to rub her hands together in anticipation of the competition. "All right, then that gives us an even number. Girls against the guys?"

Stephanie was lining up the green houses and red hotels. "Are you sure?" she asked, patting the empty space on the floor beside her. She looked disappointed. "Greg ordered chicken wings, and they're supposed to be *really* good here."

Sydney smiled but shook her head. "Maybe another night. I'm in the mood for a run. I'm weird like that—when my body takes a hit, I want to prove that I'm stronger than ever."

"You didn't get enough exercise today, huh?" Paul asked, sitting on the floor and leaning his back against a couch. He had the little metal top hat game piece on his pinkie.

"I want to make sure I'm thoroughly exhausted," Sydney joked. "Get my money's worth from this trip."

She wasn't surprised that Paul thought her reason for running was for exercise. Most people made that mistake.

The fact was, Sydney simply loved to run. Francie was always telling her that she was in great shape, that she didn't need to run as much as she did. That was because Francie wasn't a runner (or a swimmer or a cyclist, for that matter). She didn't really understand the nature of the sport. What Sydney loved about running wasn't so much the physical benefits, though that was part of it. Instead, it was the competition: with other runners, like her friend Todd from track, and with herself.

After a few minutes of leg lifts and other warm-up exercises in the hotel parking lot, Sydney headed out onto the bike path-cum-jogging trail that ran alongside the main boulevard. Before she became an agent, the idea of running by herself in a strange place would have made her nervous. But now, after almost a year of training that included self-defense and a variety of martial arts, Sydney had no doubt that she could more than protect herself against anyone unlucky enough to pick her as a target.

As her sneakers thudded against the pavement, Sydney's mind wandered back to the rock-climbing expedition. She knew she could have been hurt, really hurt, if not for her quick thinking and Paul's stepping in to save her. But there was something more on her mind.

Why was Stephanie so upset? she wondered, blowing a strand of brown hair from her face. *I know she likes me and wouldn't want to see me hurt, but it was almost like she was scared for her own safety.*

Stephanie was the one who was supposed to have been in the harness. Would she have managed to grab that tree root if she had been in Sydney's place? *Or maybe Chris was wrong and I did mess up,* Sydney thought. She'd never know for sure.

But Stephanie's blurted-out comment kept racing through her mind. . . . *It should have been me. . . . Someone wanted this to happen. . . .* It was as if her roommate thought she had avoided some predetermined outcome by switching places with Sydney.

Chris had thoroughly checked the equipment and found nothing wrong.

So how could her accident have happened? Did someone tamper with the equipment, as Stephanie had tearfully mumbled—someone so good at it that Chris couldn't even detect a problem?

As her muscles loosened and warmed, Sydney regulated her breathing and continued down the bike path. She wasn't going to worry about sabotage. She had seen how meticulous Stephanie was in everything she did—not to mention how ready she'd been to believe that someone had compromised their room.

Maybe it was just in her nature not to trust people. Given her mother's death and her father's cool demeanor, Sydney knew just how difficult it could be to do that.

Stephanie was just overreacting, Sydney decided, following the bike path as it wended its way through a grove of trees and over a footbridge. It was just an honest accident—one that she'd just as soon put behind her. She closed her eyes for a second, letting the cool evening air sweep over her clammy skin.

Her best guess told her that she'd easily covered her first mile by now.

By the time she'd completed her second, any thoughts she'd had about someone undermining the day's events were swept free, replaced by the methodical thud of running shoes hitting blacktop, the sound of cicadas chirping hidden in the trees.

*   *   *

The Maple Leaf Lodge was quiet when she got back, the lobby deserted except for the check-in clerk, who gave her a tired wave as he sat hunched over a crossword puzzle.

"I wonder if they saved me a chicken wing," Sydney said to herself as she walked down the interior hall to her room. "Not that we have anyplace to heat it up, but—"

"What the hell are you talking about?" came a loud male voice from around the corner.

Sydney couldn't make out what the female voice said in return, but whoever it was, was crying.

"That's so typical. Turn on the waterworks at

the most minor thing." Now the man sounded like he was approaching where she was standing.

Looking quickly around, Sydney ducked into the ice-machine area. Getting caught in a romantic quarrel was not how she wanted to end her evening.

"So you tell me. Why do things like that keep happening? You're saying I'm just imagining it?" the girl managed to say between sobs.

Sydney shrank back as someone punched the wall. "You know what?" the guy went on. "You're crazy. Crazy! And I'm tired of it, Stephanie. If you know what's good for you, you'll back off."

Sydney blinked, her heart pounding. *Stephanie?*

"I'm not kidding," the voice that Sydney now recognized as Paul's continued. "So don't push it."

Sydney pressed her back against the wall and listened as Paul strode past her down the hall.

What the hell was that all about?

Sydney waited until she was sure Paul was gone, and then waited a few minutes more to give Stephanie a chance to compose herself.

She walked the twenty feet to her room and made a big production of retrieving her card key from her waist pack. "Where is your key when you really need it?" she said loudly, adding a cough or two to make her presence known. At last, she inserted the card key into the slot, the green light lit, and she pushed the door open.

"Hello? Anyone home?" she called, glancing over at the sitting area near the TV.

"You missed a butt-kicking game of Monopoly." Stephanie stood in the bathroom doorway clad in a huge white towel. Droplets of water glistened on her arms, and her long blond hair was wrapped up turban-style on top of her head. Her face was only a tiny bit blotchy, easily explained by a hot shower.

"I did?" Sydney said, swallowing. Obviously her roommate wasn't going to let on that anything had just occurred.

Stephanie grinned. "Yep. Maureen was the Donald Trump of board games. She brought Greg and Paul to their knees."

"Speaking of Paul, is he around?" Sydney said, watching Stephanie's face carefully. "I thought I heard a guy's voice when I was walking down the hall."

"Nope. Just me." Then Stephanie laughed. "Maybe you heard me singing Broadway show tunes in the shower. I'm so off-key, karaoke bars close when they see me coming."

A large red welt was swelling on Stephanie's left shoulder. "No—no, I don't think that was what

I heard," Sydney stammered, her eyes glued to the bruise.

Stephanie followed Sydney's gaze. "Silly me," Stephanie said, taking her robe down from the bathroom hook and slipping it on. "I spend the whole day doing death-defying moves on the rock wall and then stumble when I get inside the shower stall." She gave her forehead a mock slap. "Bonehead with a capital *B*."

"Do you want me to get some ice?" Sydney offered. *I know right where the ice machine is,* she thought, swallowing. "It might help stop the swelling."

Stephanie shook her head. "No, I'll be fine." She rolled her blue eyes. "I'm infamous for my klutz moves back in the dorm."

But as Stephanie went back into the bathroom and turned on the blow-dryer, Sydney wasn't so sure about that.

Bonehead? Klutz? Uh-uh. Sydney wasn't buying that for a minute.

She walked over and sat on the bed, slowly unlacing her sneakers.

What was going on between Stephanie and Paul?

7

AFTER BAGELS AND HAZELNUT coffee on Friday morning, Sydney was eager to finally have the chance to check out the falls. She was hoping for an opportunity to break off from the group and look for Sanderling's notes. *This is my third day here— I've got to get moving!* she'd scolded herself as she'd put on a pair of shorts and a navy blue polo shirt. She hadn't given Sanderling more than a cursory thought since her arrival, and that had to change. And she had wondered again if she was the only agent to have a mission. So far, no one was sharing any details.

For now, she and Stephanie walked with the rest of the group, minus Agents Henry and Sinclair, covering the considerable distance from the lodge down the Niagara Parkway, which led straight to the falls. Stephanie had worn a white shirt with three-quarter-length sleeves, so there was no way to see if the welt Sydney had noticed the night before had turned into a full-fledged bruise.

Just forget it, Sydney told herself as her room-mate bounced along beside her, her hair in a tight braid, her cheeks glowing. *If she wanted you to know about it, she'd tell you.*

Waist-high metal railings lined the vast viewing area on the Canadian side of the falls, and despite the early hour, there were already hundreds of tourists milling about, cameras and camcorders in tow. Large manicured grounds bloomed with flowers, and shuttle buses dropped people off along the scenic route. Sydney leaned against a railing and gazed out over the Horseshoe Falls as the water thundered around them.

"It makes you feel pretty small, doesn't it?" Stephanie said from beside her as the mist rising from the roaring water deep below coated their skin. "Insignificant."

Sydney nodded, her toes perched on the small curb below the railing. They were on a steep cliff that dropped sharply down to the water. "Can you believe that people actually went over Niagara Falls in barrels? Now that's insane."

"And they lived," Paul chimed in, running his hand through his damp hair. "I read that a woman in her sixties voluntarily took the plunge in a barrel. Even more insane."

"No one has ever survived going over the American Falls," Stephanie said, gazing down at the gorge. "With or without a safety device."

Maureen took out her camera and snapped a picture. "For once I'll have a souvenir of a trip."

"See that boat down there?" Greg said, walking over to them. Sydney could see a blue and white boat bobbing in the turbulent water. "That's the *Maid of the Mist*. I remember riding it as a kid on vacation with my family."

The closest Sydney and her father had ever come to a vacation was when he took her to Disneyland when she was eight. He'd ridden It's a Small World and the Matterhorn with a grim smile plastered on his face, his body stiff with discomfort. Sydney couldn't wait for the day to end.

"See that gift shop over there?" Sydney asked, pointing to a large brick building several hundred yards behind them. She was itching to get to work.

"I'm going to go check it out. I'll catch up with you later."

"I'll come," Stephanie said, pushing a wet strand of hair from her cheek. "I need to dry off."

And within seconds Sydney's plan to sneak off was effectively over as the entire group joined her on a bathroom stop/postcard-buying expedition.

"We've got a little time left," Maureen announced, checking her watch twenty minutes later. "Let's go up Clifton Hill." Clifton Hill was an area filled with chain motels, low-quality high-priced restaurants, and plenty of tacky gift shops.

"Can you say tourist trap?" Greg asked as they walked slowly uphill, stopping in front of a store selling miniature barrels and maple-leaf magnets.

"I know it's cheesy, but I have to admit I think it's fun," Sydney said, fingering a light blue T-shirt that said YOURS UNTIL NIAGARA FALLS.

"My friend Ingrid would love that shirt," Stephanie said wistfully.

"Not like we can bring home souvenirs, though," Sydney said, resignedly putting the shirt back in its pile.

"Hey, guys, check this out," Paul called, motioning to them to catch up. He stood in front of a garishly decorated gray storefront. A skeleton stood on one side of the doorway, while on the other was a purple octopus. Inside the cavelike entrance was an admission booth, with a sign that read, THE WILD! THE WACKY! THE UTTERLY GHOULISH! ALL IN DELUXE WAX FORMATION. ONLY $8.00 PER PERSON! above it.

"Eight bucks for this?" Maureen said skeptically, poking the skeleton with her finger.

"Eight bucks Canadian," Greg clarified. "That's only six real dollars."

"Our Canadian friends wouldn't like to hear you say that." Maureen *tsk-tsk*ed.

"Whoever's dollar it is, it's my treat," Paul said, pulling out his wallet and handing several twenties to the cashier.

Sydney was stepping forward to go in with the others when she realized Stephanie was pulling back. "Come on, it'll be a goof," she told her.

Stephanie hesitated. "I'm—I'm not really into this kind of thing."

"I would die for my country, but please don't make me go into a haunted house," Greg mocked, clasping his hands as if in prayer.

Paul touched Stephanie's arm. "Don't worry. The ghosts and ghouls only come out at night."

Sydney watched as Stephanie gave Paul a frosty look. "I guess there's nothing to worry about then," she said, sidestepping him and grabbing Sydney's hand.

There was definitely something going on between them. *I wish Stephanie would fill me in,* Sydney thought restlessly. *I could tell her about Noah and we could compare notes on having boyfriends who happen to work for the CIA.*

Shaking off her thoughts, Sydney stepped inside the haunted house. The air was stuffy and moist, and it was difficult to see as they navigated through the twisting turns.

"Looks like we lost them," Sydney said, peering over her shoulder in the dark. "Do you want to wait?"

"And get teased at every turn?" Stephanie sniffed as they shuffled along. Weird moldy wax creatures sat behind iron bars, their ghoulish faces twisted into evil grins. "No, thanks."

"You know, we could kick some serious wax monster butt in here," Sydney said under her breath as a couple of boisterous boys pushed past them. "I mean, how often do five CIA agents hang out in a place like this?"

"Mm-hmm," came Stephanie's voice. She did not sound at all happy. *In fact, she sounds like she might cry,* Sydney thought, moving up a few uneven steps.

"Blaa-ha-ha!" A thin skeleton screeched at the top of the stairwell, his bony face lighting up with a pale green glow.

Stephanie stumbled back. "Ow!" she muttered, banging her head on a low part of the ceiling. "Did I say that I hate places like this?"

"No . . . but it's kind of obvious."

"What was that?" Stephanie blurted out as a moaning wail echoed down the corridor. "Can you see Paul or Greg?"

"I think they went the other way," Sydney said as they came out into a large windowless room lit by several flickering wall sconces.

"I want to stay far away from them," Stephanie said adamantly. "They'd love to scare the crap out of me."

"You know what's really scary?" Sydney pointed to the ceiling. "Those massive spiderwebs are probably real."

Stephanie wrapped her arms around herself. "Let's find the exit."

It was funny. Sydney would bet that Stephanie had held her own against assailants ranging from drug lords to arms dealers—that was just a part of life as a special agent. So why was she so spooked over the tawdry special effects in a Niagara Falls funhouse?

They entered another dank corridor. Large plastic bats were suspended from the ceiling. "I'm sure this is someone's idea of fun," Sydney said, brushing one of them aside. "But to be honest, it's not exactly mine." Instead of traipsing through the haunted house, she needed to start her search for Sanderling's notes. It seemed like an easy enough mission, but if it wasn't, she wanted to make sure she'd have enough time to complete it.

"Oh!" Stephanie shrieked as a pair of rubbery hands reached through a hole in the wall and tried to grab her. Instead, she grabbed them back and twisted.

"Ow!" The rubbery hands jerked back inside their hole.

"I, uh, I think you may have hurt him," Sydney said worriedly as the person behind the wall let out some choice words.

Stephanie pushed past Sydney. "I *need* to get out of here. Right now."

There was no mistaking the unease in her voice. Sydney followed her, and to her relief, they were soon pushing through a door into the bright sunshine outside.

"What took you guys so long?" Maureen asked, hopping up from the bench she was sitting on with Greg.

Sydney squinted as her eyes adjusted to the daylight. "Oh, you know. Shooting the breeze with a few ghouls is always so time-consuming." She turned to Stephanie, expecting her to make a joke. But her friend looked visibly shaken.

"Is Paul with you?" Stephanie asked, her eyes darting around the street.

Greg laughed. "Nah, I think he was hoping to terrorize you two a little in there."

"We could always grant him his wish," Sydney joked.

But Stephanie's face was pale. "If you think I'm setting foot inside that place again, you're not as smart as I thought you were."

* * *

In order to immerse the agents in French Canadian culture, Agent Henry had announced that Friday night would be spent at a local vineyard for a premium wine tasting. That was why Sydney was dressed in the nicest outfit she'd brought, a sleeveless light blue dress that Francie always said made her eyes shine, and matching leather sandals, sitting in a cast-iron chair on the patio of the Lake de Luc Vineyard.

Paul and Stephanie were sitting next to each

other under an umbrella-shaded table. Sydney had noticed that Stephanie had been avoiding him all day, so she was surprised to see them together now. Whatever the spat of the night before had been about had obviously been forgotten. They were nibbling cubes of cheese and clinking their glasses together.

Or maybe they've had a little too much wine, Sydney thought, smiling. Her roommate was glowing in a brightly patterned floral halter dress, a lightweight cardigan draped over her shoulders. And Paul was the picture of attentiveness, pulling out her chair and dabbing at her mouth with his napkin.

"Fine wine is grown and not made," Pierre Comte, the vineyard's owner, proclaimed from behind an outdoor bar lined with full, round wineglasses for red wine, and tall, slender ones for white. He had just finished taking them on a tour of the property and was busily assembling a variety of wines for the agents to sample.

Sydney had been charmed by the lovely scenery as prearranged limousines had driven them to the picturesque town of Niagara-on-the-Lake. She had grown up in California, but she'd never actually visited a vineyard. "If all the vineyards back home are as beautiful as this one, I'm going to book a trip immediately," Sydney said now as Pierre handed out glasses one quarter filled with a deep red wine.

"On all those free weekends we have, right?" Maureen cracked from the seat next to her.

"Merlot," Pierre announced as everyone took a drink of wine, murmuring appreciatively. A pinot grigio followed, then a zinfandel. Sydney was careful to take only small sips and made sure she sampled the crackers and cheese that were offered as well. She definitely did not need to have a headache.

She was tasting some Riesling when she noticed Paul slowly stand up, rubbing his temples. His face had turned a pasty white.

"Are you all right?" Pierre asked, his brow creasing with concern. "Perhaps you should have a bite to eat. Some bread or cheese."

Paul smiled weakly. "Thanks, but I'm going to catch a cab back to the hotel," he said, setting his barely touched wineglass on the table. "My head is killing me."

Sydney glanced over at Stephanie. If they were indeed a couple and things were good, wouldn't she offer to go with him? But when she didn't, Sydney felt obligated to speak up. "Do you want one of us to come with you?"

"Nah, I don't want to spoil it for you guys. I'll

be fine." After Paul had said his good-byes, Pierre called a cab for him and minutes later he was gone.

"Eat, eat," Pierre urged, passing around a platter of fresh fruit kebobs. "I want you to enjoy, not equate my vineyard with a migraine."

"Paul gets headaches a lot," Stephanie said, looking off in the direction he had walked.

"I guess you know a lot about him," Sydney said as Greg and Maureen went over and sat at the bar and began inspecting the various bottles. The wine was making her bolder than she normally would be.

"Well, we work in the same office. . . . You know how it is," Stephanie said, tracing the rim of her glass with her finger.

Noah's twinkling eyes and wry grin flashed into Sydney's brain. "I know exactly how it is," she acknowledged, finishing the Riesling. Suddenly, she couldn't stand it anymore. She had to tell someone about Noah. And Stephanie wasn't just anyone.

Sydney was pretty sure she was in the exact same situation.

Even though she had only known Stephanie for a few days, Sydney felt a powerful connection. Their childhoods, their careers—even their choices of boyfriends.

It's like we were destined to become friends,

Sydney decided. "I—I'm dating someone at SD-6," she blurted out.

Stephanie stared at her. "You are?"

Sydney nodded, the details of her relationship with Noah over the past year now slipping effortlessly from her tongue. "It's the most exhilarating and exasperating experience I've ever had," she finished with a sheepish expression on her face.

"Wait, isn't that supposed to be what this trip is?" Stephanie said, smiling as Pierre passed out fresh wineglasses filled with a newly uncorked white wine.

"No, wait, I'm confusing myself with Greg's ex-girlfriend," Sydney said with a laugh. After a few minutes of uninhibited giggling, Sydney held up her hand. "Wait. Enough of this. Now that I've fessed up, you've got to come clean."

"About what?" Stephanie asked, her tipsy laughter subsiding.

"Come on!" Sydney laughed. "That hug on the rocks yesterday—you can't tell me that you and Paul aren't a couple."

Stephanie bit her lip and looked down at the patio. Her blue eyes grew serious. "Please don't say anything, Sydney," she said, lowering her voice. "At SD-6 maybe they don't care if agents hook up with each other, but at SD-2—"

"Are you kidding?" Sydney interrupted. "Sloane would, well . . ." She shook her head. "He would not like it, that's for sure." *And neither would have Wilson,* she thought sadly, thinking back to the handler she'd regarded as almost a father before he had betrayed SD-6.

"I'm just glad to talk to someone who's in the same boat," Sydney confessed. "And believe me, Noah and I have had some doozies of arguments too."

The blank look on Stephanie's face made Sydney blink. "You know," she said, her voice dropping even lower than it had been. "I heard you guys last night," she clarified, her tone coaxing. "You don't have to pretend about it with me."

But Stephanie's face gave away nothing. "I'm not sure what you're getting at."

Maybe Stephanie isn't as ready to talk about her romance as I am. "Oh, well, I mean, like any couple, I'm sure you guys have your moments, right?" Sydney spluttered. Obviously Stephanie didn't want to let on that she and Paul had had a fight the other night.

A major fight.

And she ended up with a big red welt.

* * *

All Sydney wanted to do was flop on the motel-room bed, dress, sandals, and mascara in place, and crash. Even though she knew she had drunk, at most, three full glasses of wine, there was a persistent buzzing in her head that wouldn't go away.

"I'll take a few aspirin and I'll be good as new," she mumbled, reaching for her cosmetic bag on the vanity. But the bag wasn't there.

"Have you seen my cosmetic bag?" she called to Stephanie, who was getting into her pajamas.

"It's on the nightstand," Stephanie said as Sydney walked into the room.

And it was. *That's weird,* Sydney thought, reaching for the case.

And what was weirder was that she could have sworn she had left her hairbrush on the night-stand—but it was on her bed. *And didn't I hang up my cardigan?* Her favorite J. Crew sweater was draped over an armchair.

"Is something wrong?" Stephanie asked, picking up on Sydney's bewilderment as she turned down the covers on her bed.

"Nothing that a few aspirin can't cure," Sydney said, taking the plastic bottle out of the bag and giving it a little shake.

Better not to say anything about her belongings being moved.

Because other than Agents Henry and Sinclair, there was only one person who would have had access to their room that night. A person who had left the Lake de Luc Vineyard early.

And I'm definitely not going to open that Pandora's box.

8

"I THOUGHT YOU ORDERED an omelet," Maureen said, eyeing Greg's large white platter.

Greg used his fork to flip the large folded-over yellow pancake, shards of overdone bacon spilling from the inside. "I did."

Stephanie ripped open a miniature box of Corn Flakes and poured it into her cereal bowl. "At least they can't really mess this up."

Sydney took a sip of orange juice. Everyone had received their orders except for her, and judging by the reaction the food was getting, she wasn't too sure how big her appetite was going to be. They were eating breakfast together in the hotel's spacious restaurant before their first French lesson began later that morning. Large windows lined the rear, letting in streams of early sunlight, and patrons were beginning to fill the room.

Everyone in their group was present except Paul. Greg had said the Chicago agent still wasn't feeling well when he came down for breakfast. "Guess he's more of a beer man," Greg said with a shrug.

Sydney had tried to gauge Stephanie's reaction to Paul's absence, but her friend's expression remained void of any emotion. *I could learn a few things from her,* Sydney thought. Whenever Noah was near her at SD-6, Sydney was certain that her face became an emotional barometer.

Beep-beep! Beep-beep! Four pairs of hands immediately reached for pagers.

"It's me," Sydney said as Graham's number back at headquarters appeared on the small gray screen. She pulled her cell phone from her khaki shorts pocket and punched in his number.

"Hey, Sydney. How's it going?" Graham's familiar voice came over the line.

"Okay. What's up?"

"Look, there might be a problem," Graham blurted out, suddenly rushing his words. Sydney could tell he was nervous. "Those digital camera gloves I gave you? Well, they have a glitch."

Sydney frowned. "What kind of glitch?"

"I'm not exactly sure yet. What I need you to do is run them through your personal scanner." Sydney had taken one in her luggage, but it wasn't always reliable. Sometimes it took three tries to get it to work properly.

"Okay," she said. "I'll do it right now. Call me back if you need anything else." Just as she pushed her chair back, the waitress deposited a steaming plate of scrambled eggs, sausages, and toast.

"Now that looks good," Greg said enviously.

Sydney sighed and pushed her chair back from the table. "Go ahead and help yourself. I might be a while."

* * *

It's not fair, Sydney thought as she trudged down the worn Berber carpet to her room. *I deserved those eggs and sausages.*

She slipped her card key in and pushed open the door—and froze. A man wearing black pants, a dark sweatshirt, and a ski mask was inside, in the middle of rifling through the room!

Instinctively she tossed her bag to the side as the intruder rushed toward her. Throwing her arm up to block a blow, she reared back and gave him a quick kick in the ribs.

He doubled over, but only for a second. He then let loose with his own flying side kick, narrowly missing Sydney's face. She tumbled over the bed to avoid being pinned against the wall, and before she could blink he had picked up an empty suitcase.

He charged hard at her with it, knocking her to the floor. Taking advantage of Sydney's momentary out-of-commission status, he snatched a small tool bag from the floor, and then he was out of the motel room and flying down the hall.

The good news was that apparently he wasn't a psychopath bent on assaulting a female coed in her motel room.

The bad news was that he was a thief. *But of what?* Sydney thought, scrambling to her feet and taking off after him.

He raced down the carpeted interior hallway and Sydney was on his heels, her heart pounding and adrenaline coursing through her veins. If she had known she was going to encounter a fleet-footed burglar, she would have worn her track shoes instead of the fashionable but impossible-to-run-in chunky black sandals that were slowing her to a hobble.

This guy is fast, she realized as he barreled out the door at the end of the corridor into the daylight-filled parking lot. *And in these shoes, I am definitely not.*

"Why in the world did I let Francie talk me into buying these?" she yelled in frustration, stopping to yank them from her feet.

But in the time she'd taken to stop and remove her sandals, the man had increased the distance between them to the point that Sydney realized he was going to get away. "Unhhh!" Desperate to do something, she lobbed one of the now-hated sandals at his head and seconds later heard a satisfying *whunk* as it made contact.

But it didn't slow him down.

Angry, frustrated, and barefoot, Sydney retrieved her sandals, put them back on, and marched back to the lodge.

Should she report this to Agent Henry or Agent Sinclair? Or should she call SD-6? What if the intruder was looking for something specific to Sydney's mission? Or to Stephanie's, if she had one? What if someone had been in their room the night before, and what if that someone was the same person?

What if it was Paul?

There were way too many questions for her to answer at nine a.m.

I'll call Sloane, she decided. Her handler would know what to do.

But he wasn't in. She left him a short voice mail message and then stared at the ransacked room in front of her. Clothes lay scattered across the bed, her cosmetic bag was dumped out, and bath towels were thrown on the floor. It was impossible to know if anything of Stephanie's was missing, and without a fingerprint kit, there wasn't much she could do on her own.

He definitely was looking for something, she thought, glancing over at the wad of untouched cash Stephanie had left on the nightstand. *A petty thief would have snatched that up in a heartbeat.*

As quickly as she could, she put away her belongings, and then carefully removed from her suitcase the devices Graham had created for her. She gave them a cursory glance. Everything *seemed* okay. But she wanted to make sure. She ran the scan as per Graham's instructions and then punched in his number on her cell.

"Hi, Sydney," Graham said, clicking on the other end of the phone. "Took you long enough."

Sydney counted to five, then spoke. "How does everything look? Did you find a glitch?"

"It'll take a few hours to complete the scan. We'll just let the computer do its thing."

"Okay." Sydney looked over her gadgets again. There was no point telling Graham about the break-in. If something was wrong, his scan would tell them. "You know, we never talked about my disguise," she said thoughtfully. "Did Sloane stipulate anything to you?" Sometimes handlers gave agents specific requirements, but often they were on their own. Sydney wasn't sure which she liked better: having someone do the thinking for her or having the freedom to create her own alias, no matter how outlandish.

"No, Syd. I think you're on your own for this one," Graham told her. "Why don't you pick something up at the hotel?"

"Like what?" Sydney asked uncertainly.

"Don't they have dress shops there? What's that popular one at Caesars in Vegas . . . Versace?"

Sydney snorted. Really, if some of the people back at HQ actually went *on* a mission instead of being sequestered back in their comfy little quarters, maybe they'd have a better idea of how hard this job really was. "Any noncouture ideas?"

"Well . . . what about a maid's uniform?" Graham suggested.

Sydney had a feeling he was only half kidding. She squeezed her eyes shut. "I'm going to pretend I didn't hear that."

9

"ON EMPLOIE EN AVEC les noms de pays masculins à voyelle initiale," Madame LeFèvre said, passing out sheets of paper filled with geographical names and the corresponding French rule for preposition usage.

Taking a refresher course in French grammar in a small room at the Maple Leaf Lodge wasn't exactly how Sydney wanted to spend her weekend. French had become one of her favorite languages since she'd begun studying it in earnest the past fall. But it was lots more fun actually using it in real conversations instead of the stilted dialogue she was yawningly engaging in here.

"Israel is masculine. *En Israël.* But Mexico isn't and you still use *en. En Mexique.* Right?" Maureen whispered from the chair beside her, jabbing at her paper with her pen. "French always mixes me up. Give me something nice and easy, like Japanese. No sweat."

"It's *au Mexique,*" Sydney replied automatically. "All countries that end in *e* are feminine except for Mexico. You use *au* for masculine countries that begin with a consonant."

"This is all completely pointless," Greg complained with a sigh. "We could learn this with a click of a button on our tutorial language programs back in our home offices."

As Madame LeFèvre prattled on, Sydney was only half listening. Why had that intruder invaded their room? More importantly, who was it? He hadn't taken any of their valuables—jewelry, money, and Graham's high-tech gadgets had all been left untouched. Stephanie had been very upset when Sydney had taken her aside and quietly told her what had happened. She had methodically gone through all her personal effects in their room after breakfast. Nothing seemed to be missing.

Sydney snuck a peek over at Paul. He was scribbling something down in his notebook, an earnest expression on his face. The night before, he had left the vineyard early—and Sydney was convinced someone had been in their room. That day, he had been the only one not down for breakfast— and a masked intruder had broken in.

Are these just coincidences, or is Paul Riley involved in this in some way? His absences were starting to seem a bit too convenient.

Then she glanced over at Stephanie, who was aimlessly twirling and untwirling a long lock of blond hair around her finger. *And what does it mean for Stephanie if he is?*

"Mademoiselle Bristow!" Madame LeFèvre gave Sydney a look that said this wasn't the first time she had called her name. *"Où allez-vous?"*

Um, space? Sydney wanted to say. Instead, she smiled weakly at the stern-faced teacher. "Um . . . *je vais à Rome, Madame?"* she tried, guessing at the right answer. If this was a quiz she was going to be toast. *French* toast. *"C'est magnifique."*

Madame LeFèvre regarded Sydney with a raised eyebrow, and Sydney knew she had squeaked her way out of that one. *"Ah, oui. Rome. C'est bon."* Then she looked at the clock and snapped her fingers. *"Maintenant, mes amis, dix minutes."*

The others stirred in their seats. Sydney pushed her chair back and hurried out the door before anyone could stop her, especially an irate Madame LeFèvre.

The ladies' room was just down the hallway, and Sydney locked herself in a stall and leaned against the cold metal door. She didn't like being suspicious of the people around her. It gave her an uneasy, unsettled feeling.

She heard the outside door open, and footsteps entered the stall beside her.

"Syd?"

Sydney blinked. It was Stephanie. "Yes?"

Underneath the stall door fluttered Stephanie's fingers. "Here."

"What—" Sydney began to say as Stephanie shoved a crumpled piece of notebook paper under the partition and let it drop to the floor.

"You've got to read this," she pleaded, her voice low and shaky. "Please." The toilet in Stephanie's stall flushed, and seconds later Sydney heard the door to the hallway open and close.

Sydney picked up the paper. On it was a Web site address, www.sd2medical.org/patients/hist. She memorized the address, then reflexively shredded the paper into bits, letting the tiny scraps drop into the toilet.

She checked her watch. Only five minutes left before she had to return to the classroom. There had to be someplace in the hotel to get online, she decided. *And I'm a spy. I sure as heck should be able to find it.*

Back in the hall, she checked to make sure no one in her group saw her. The coast was clear. She walked briskly over to the hotel registration office. It was deserted. The cold cup of coffee sitting on the desk told her that whoever was supposed to be manning the post had been gone for a while.

"Let's hope he stays away for just a few more minutes," Sydney muttered, slipping in front of the unoccupied computer screen and letting her fingers whiz over the keyboard.

www.sd2medical.org/patients/hist was a medical site affiliated with a hospital in New York City. Patient names, referrals, procedures all whizzed by her eyes as she clicked open and scanned the various screens. What had Stephanie wanted her to see?

MEDICAL RECORDS OF HARLING, STEPHANIE P.

Looked like this was it.

Sydney double-clicked the icon next to Stephanie's name and a list of dates and descriptions of services popped up on the screen.

Date of Service: 4/5 Two broken ribs.

Date of Service: 4/24 Shattered cheekbone. Broken left arm. Black eye (right).

Date of Service: 5/7 Trauma to the head. Laceration above right eye. Swelling noted on lip/upper mouth area. Patient kept overnight for observation.

Sydney's eyes flew over the list of injuries Stephanie had suffered. She knew from her own experience at SD-6 that the line of work they were in made physical exams routine, and that bruises and occasional broken body parts were part of the risk they undertook every day.

But these injuries?

These were a whole other story.

At the bottom of the page was a special section labeled Remarks.

Staff Drs. Delta and Thornton believe that injuries were inflicted at the hands of suspect's boyfriend, but Ms. Harling chose not to disclose his identity. As per the request of her commanding unit's superior officer, the hospital staff elected to—

"What are you looking at?" asked a familiar, friendly-sounding voice behind Sydney, startling her from her task and making her gasp.

Slowly, she swiveled in her chair, her heart sinking like a stone . . . and saw Paul Riley standing over her, his eyes locked squarely on hers.

10

"OH, MY GOSH. I can't believe you caught me in here. This is *so* embarrassing," Sydney burst out, making sure to keep her voice confessional, her expression sheepish. She winced. "See, I went on a bit of a shopping spree at Fashion Island before I came here—you know, new clothes for the trip and all—and I've been panicking that my bank account was completely overdrawn." Sydney gestured to the computer, where, thankfully, a hockey stick and puck screen saver was flashing. "So I couldn't take it anymore. I snuck in here to look up my checking account online."

"And what did you find out?" Paul asked, sticking his hands in his shorts pockets and rocking on his heels. "Are the bank police going to be coming for you?"

Sydney made herself laugh. *If anyone needs to meet up with the police, it's you,* she thought, wishing she could break his arms after what she'd just learned. But what she said was, "Actually, I think that's them right now," as she nodded to the area behind Paul. As he turned to look, she quickly moved the mouse to eliminate the screen saver, then immediately clicked the X in the upper right-hand corner to close the screen.

"I'm good for a few more trips to the Gap," Sydney said, standing up and pushing the chair in. "Instead, we should probably start worrying about Madame LeFèvre's *gendarmes,* don't you think?"

"Yeah, she's outrageous enough to actually do that," Paul said, giving Sydney a casual grin. For now, it appeared that he bought her story completely.

That was close, Bristow, she thought as they walked back to the room.

But if the teacher thought she was a space cadet before, she was going to think Sydney was a commissioned officer now. There was no way Sydney was going to be able to concentrate on French or border regulations or immigration law or anything except the extent of Stephanie's injuries she had just uncovered online.

What's wrong with him? she thought as they took their seats. Didn't SD-2 make their agents undergo a rigorous screening process before they were recruited? Heaven knew she had been put through the wringer in Los Angeles. How could SD-2 let a psycho like Paul into the agency? *What's wrong with* them?

Sydney was at a loss as to what to do. Now more than ever, she was convinced that Paul was the one who had broken into her room.

Okay. Sydney had the information Stephanie had obviously wanted her to find.

But now that I have it, what am I supposed to do with it?

* * *

The rest of Saturday and most of Sunday was spent trailing after customs officers and learning more about how their operations were run. Sydney and Maureen were with Agent Sinclair, while Greg, Paul, and Stephanie were teamed with Agent Henry.

"So you're separating us?" Sydney had asked, dismayed, as she watched the other group pile into a waiting sedan outside the Maple Leaf Lodge.

"They're off to the Peace Bridge," Agent Sinclair explained. "You lucky ducks get to stay with me at the Rainbow Bridge." He patted his stomach. "Not only is the drive a helluva lot closer, there's a great burger joint that my buddies there have made a lunch reservation at."

"Well, if they take reservations, there's hope," Maureen had muttered as another car pulled up for them. After days of watching the burly officer only eat things that came in Styrofoam or paper takeout bags, Sydney had to agree with her.

Sydney was restless to do something concrete to find out more about Paul Riley.

But with Maureen glued to her side and a group of overeager Canadian officials keyed up to show off their operation to American CIA agents, there was nothing to do except focus on the very exciting ins and outs of immigration law.

* * *

"Okay, baby, time to take it to the streets," Sydney said to herself Sunday evening. She and Maureen had been the first ones back to the lodge. She was alone in the motel room, sitting cross-legged on her bed. For the past fifteen minutes she had gone over a detailed map of the Canadian side of Niagara Falls that she'd picked up at the front desk, along with the notes Sloane had provided her back at SD-6. According to his instructions, she should head to the Table Rock Scenic Tunnels, which lead underground to three different views of the Horseshoe Falls. There, somewhere behind wet moldy rock, she should find Sanderling's notes.

This was probably the easiest mission she'd been sent on—and the one that was taking her the longest to accomplish. "If I weren't surrounded by SD agents morning, noon, and night, I might be able to get something done," Sydney grumbled, tossing aside a coupon for free pancakes at a diner on Clifton Hill.

Just then the motel room door opened and Stephanie stepped inside.

Sydney took a deep breath. "Hey, stranger. You're back." Focusing on her mission had been a respite from all the worry she'd been shouldering over the past twenty-four hours. She hadn't allowed herself to think about Stephanie—she hadn't even seen Stephanie. Her roommate hadn't arrived back yet the night before when Sydney went to bed at eleven, and when she had woken up that morning, Stephanie was already gone. But now that the two of them were alone behind closed doors, Carl Sanderling was all but forgotten.

Stephanie's face was white. Joining Sydney on her bed, she picked up the remote and turned the TV on, the volume loud enough to cover their voices.

"I have been dying to talk to you all day," Stephanie said, tears welling up in her eyes. "I wanted to cry when Agent Henry told me to go with him. And you were sleeping so soundly last night that I didn't have the heart to wake you."

"Hey, it's not Henry's fault," Sydney said, arching her right eyebrow. "How was he to know that you'd just shown me evidence that you're a punching bag for your boyfriend, who would appear to be none other than our very own Paul Riley." Sydney knew she sounded harsh, but she couldn't help it. How could someone as sweet and smart as Stephanie get involved with someone like Paul . . . and keep going back for more? Sydney had never been able to understand girls like that.

"Sydney, look. You have to listen to me, and more than that, believe me." Stephanie swallowed.

"I—I couldn't take it any longer. That's why I gave you the Web address."

"But what do you expect me to do about it?" Sydney asked, confused.

Stephanie took a deep breath. "When I first met Paul at our SD-2 New Year's party, I thought he was really sweet. We'd passed each other in the hallway a lot, and I had had a crush on him for weeks. So I was psyched to actually get to know him in person." She looked down at her hands. "And he was really great in the beginning. Sending me flowers, little cards, you know. That sort of thing."

Sydney nodded. "But . . ."

"But then he started to change. He seemed tense all the time. He got angry with me over little things—minute things, really. And . . ." A tear trickled down Stephanie's cheek. "And he began to hit me," she said softly.

Sydney shook her head in disgust. It was hard to reconcile the abuser Stephanie was describing with the friendly, sweet-demeanored guy she'd gotten to know in the past few days, but Sydney had no doubt that Stephanie was telling the truth. And besides that, the hospital data didn't lie.

"I know I wasn't in your shoes," Sydney said, choosing her words carefully, "but to be honest, it's not like you didn't know how to defend yourself. Right?" If a guy she was dating ever tried anything like that on her, she would have him on his knees, begging for mercy.

Stephanie gave a little helpless shrug. "I know it sounds lame, but I kept thinking he was going to stop. But—but you saw the Web site. And he's getting stranger every day. He acts completely normal around everyone else . . . but with me, it's like he's another person."

Sydney sat there. She didn't know what to say. If Francie were here, she'd tell Paul to shove it . . . but then again, Francie wouldn't know the whole story.

"Things just escalated out of control," Stephanie finished. "And—and that fight you heard the other night—" She broke off, shaking her head. "I guess I'm so used to covering our arguments up to my friends and my landlord that I almost believed my story myself. You think you know someone, but then—"

A soda commercial blasted onto the TV, making them both jump. "Okay, what I'm not getting here is why you don't tell SD-2," Sydney demanded. "Surely they'd put a stop to this!"

But Stephanie looked horrified at the thought.

"Sydney, first of all, SD-2 *does* know. . . . The hospital I went to is an SD-2 hospital. Everyone there looked the other way."

"But why?" Sydney persisted. Why would SD-2 want an agent like Paul as part of the team? It didn't make sense.

Stephanie picked up a bed pillow and hugged it to her chest. She blew out her breath. "Here's where it gets really messy. Not only are agents not supposed to become romantically involved, but . . . Paul's father is—is my handler at SD-2."

"What?" Sydney cried out in disbelief.

"There's no way I can speak out against Paul without putting my life in jeopardy," Stephanie said, her voice catching.

"This is big, Stephanie," Sydney said slowly. "Really big." She sat quietly for a moment, trying to filter the completely crazy ideas floating through her mind from the semicrazy ones. Should she call Noah? Sloane? She squeezed her eyes shut at the idea of trying to explain everything to their disbelieving, disapproving ears. Not only were agents not supposed to share their personal lives with each other, agents were most definitely not to be romantically involved. Sloane was a very by-the-book person, Sydney had realized. He wouldn't want to hear about Stephanie's problems—he'd be too focused on the fact that she'd gone outside protocol by becoming intimate with Paul in the first place.

Maybe another woman could help, Sydney thought, wishing she could call Francie. Emily Sloane? *Whoa, Syd. That is beyond completely crazy.* That would be completely insane.

Sydney shook her head, trying to focus. "Stephanie, I want to help you. I really do. But how can I?" She gestured to the maps littering the bed. "I don't even know what I'm going to wear on my mission tomorrow."

Oops. Way to give up that she was on a job. But that divulgence paled in the face of what they had just been talking about.

"I have a disguise for you," Stephanie said quietly. "In fact, it's staring you right in the face."

"Huh?"

"Me," Stephanie said. "Disguise yourself as me."

Sydney gave her roommate a bewildered gaze. "Why would I want to look like you?"

"Because that's the only way you'll be able to see for yourself how Paul is when he's alone with me."

"I'm not sure I understand why that's important," Sydney said uncertainly.

"It's very important," Stephanie told her, grabbing hold of Sydney's wrists. Her hands were cold as steel and her gaze was steady. "I need you to believe me when I tell you that he's a threat, and to see it with your own eyes. Because I want Paul dead.

"And Sydney?" Stephanie swallowed. "I need you to commit the crime."

11

SYDNEY LET OUT A small gasp, then shook herself free from Stephanie's grip. "It's one thing to help you *break up* with Paul," she said firmly. "It's a completely different animal to *kill* him!"

The idea sounded like a plot hatched on a TV movie, or a real-life drama where someone hires a hit man to kill their spouse. Knowing that she had actually been trained to kill, and that such knowledge was part of life as a CIA officer, was the part of her job she disliked the most. "From the moment I joined SD-6, I have never wanted to kill anyone," she said truthfully. "I'll do it if it's in self-defense, but—" She held up her hand as Stephanie started to speak. "Obviously you are in a beyond-bad situation. But before you do something really stupid, you need to step back from this. You could come home with me, to L.A." Sydney felt certain that her superiors at SD-6 could offer Stephanie the protection she needed.

But Stephanie shook her head quickly, her face defeated. "There's no way I could do that. Paul would find me in a heartbeat." She stood up and paced nervously in front of the TV. Then she turned, sitting down on the low dresser. "I'm going to tell you something, but you must *swear* to secrecy. Swear."

Sydney gave her an incredulous look. After what they had just been talking about, was secrecy really an issue?

"Fine, I swear," Sydney said dutifully.

"A few minutes ago you said you were on a mission. . . . Well, I'm on a mission too," Stephanie admitted. "SD-2 has intel that suggests that Paul and his father are double agents working for K-Directorate."

Sydney let out a low whistle at the mention of the rogue Russian spy group. The plot was thickening.

Stephanie nodded. "Before I was sent here to

Niagara Falls, another, more high-ranking officer stepped in and asked me to spy on Paul and to secure any information I can about him."

"Who was the agent?" Sydney asked.

"I'm not at liberty to say," Stephanie told her reluctantly. "To make things easier, I'll call him . . . Jones. Jones had no idea that I'd been romantically involved with Paul. But we only were together for a few weeks before I realized I'd made the biggest mistake of my life." Stephanie put her face in her hands.

"And so now—" Sydney prompted gently.

"Now I've been asked by Jones to eliminate Paul should I be able to confirm his double-agent status." Stephanie held up her thumb and pointer finger millimeters apart. "And I'm *this close* to having the proof I need." She stood up abruptly. "I've never killed anybody," she confessed, her blue eyes pooling with tears. "But I'm not afraid to do it if that's what I'm ordered to do."

Sydney sat for a minute, trying to absorb it all. When she'd first heard Stephanie's plan, it sounded like out-and-out murder. But now, with K-Directorate and Jones involved, it wasn't nearly as cut and dried.

"The big problem, though, is that if something happens to Paul and I can be pinned to the crime,

Paul's father will see to it that I'm eliminated." Stephanie's eyes were pleading. "So I need someone to help me. And—and you're the only one I trust."

The wheels had been spinning in Sydney's head. Knowing that Stephanie really trusted her made it awfully hard to tell her no. *I'd hate to think that if I turned to someone I trusted for help, they'd turn me away,* Sydney thought, her emotions churning inside her.

"It's not that I don't believe you," Sydney began, "but it's a lot to deal with. I—I'm not sure what to say."

Stephanie came over and sat down next to her. Gone was the bubbly blond beauty who had strode into the Maple Leaf Lodge just a few days before. In her place was a scared, thin, wide-eyed girl . . . a girl who had become a friend.

A surge of pity rushed through Sydney as she tried to imagine herself in Stephanie's situation. And in truth, it wasn't as if Stephanie was committing a crime—if Paul was a double agent, she'd be doing her duty as an officer of the U.S. government.

"I guess—it's just that I can't believe we're actually having a conversation about *killing* someone. . . . I'm a college sophomore, for Pete's sake," Sydney said at last.

Stephanie let out a wry laugh. "We should be worrying about what classes to take and which happy hours to go to, not plotting the death of a K-Directorate agent, right?"

Sydney managed a small smile. "Exactly." She pushed herself off the bed and picked up her card key from the nightstand. "I need to go for a walk and think a little bit. Okay?"

Stephanie nodded. "Thanks, Sydney. Even— even if you can't help me, it means a lot to me that you were willing to listen . . . and believe me."

Walking down the corridor, Sydney focused her thoughts. She did believe Stephanie was telling the truth. But whether she wanted to get involved . . . that was another story.

Still, how could she walk away, knowing that SD-2 might be home to a double agent and that a fellow agent was in serious jeopardy?

Before she realized it, she was turning down the wing where Paul and Greg's room was located. She slowed as she passed their door, the chance to do a little reconnaissance eating away at her. She was pretty sure she could find a way to break into the room—but what would that solve? And explaining it to Agent Henry if she was caught would take some real doing.

Instead, she headed for the lobby. On impulse,

she bought a bottle of water and a bag of chips from a vending machine, then stepped outside. The cool evening air washed over her, and for a moment, she wished she had changed into her running clothes.

Instead, she turned down Niagara Parkway and headed toward the falls. *Maybe I'll ride up the Skylon Tower,* she thought, wondering if the elevated view of the falls would show her anything that might help her make a decision.

I could always go to one of the nightclubs on Clifton Hill, she thought, smiling as she walked down the dark street, lit every few hundred yards with a streetlamp. The drinking age in Ontario was nineteen. *I'd be completely legal. Wouldn't the frat guys back home love to go to school here!* But it wouldn't be much fun sitting in a bar without any of her friends to hang out with.

She wished she could see the Festival of Lights she had read about in a tourist guidebook. Starting in late autumn the city of Niagara Falls lit up the water with rainbow-colored lights, using so many strings of lightbulbs that it was well into January before they could get them all down.

At the pace she was keeping, she'd be at the falls in a few minutes.

What would Noah do? she wondered as the air around her grew moist and her ears picked up the dull roar of the water. Well, one thing was for sure. He definitely wouldn't be wondering what *she* would do. For better or worse, he would react.

She was standing next to a large framed map of the Canadian Falls, trying to decide where to go, when she heard someone call her name.

"Hey!" she exclaimed, jogging over to where Maureen was sitting on a bench, her hair pulled into a short stubby ponytail. "What's going on?"

"Paul and I were just hanging out," Maureen said, patting the empty seat beside her. "He had to visit the rest room." She shivered. "And he promised to bring back some coffee too."

"Oh!" Sydney said, barely believing her good luck. "I'll go see if I can find him and make that two cups."

"Make sure he grabs three sugars," Maureen called as Sydney started up the embankment toward the visitors' center.

Sydney didn't plan on letting Paul see her, but maybe she'd catch him doing something that would be helpful in some way. Like . . . like . . . *Like what, Sydney? Coming out of the men's room? Grabbing four sugars?* Well, she was stumped.

But the chance to see him after all Stephanie had told her was too tempting to pass up. Making her way up the sidewalk, Sydney passed tourists taking in the falls at night. A quick look inside the visitors' center told her that Paul wasn't there, and the coffee shop was empty save for a group of German tourists. Sydney hesitated under the green-awninged portico of the shop and suddenly picked up the sound of Russian being spoken in the darkness alongside the building.

Sydney walked away from the building and moved behind a large kiosk. There was a pay phone adjacent to the visitors' center, and a man was hunched beside it, talking quietly into the phone.

Stealthily, Sydney inched her way around the kiosk, trying to get within earshot without alerting the man to her presence.

Squinting in the darkness, she recognized Paul's tall frame and his messy hair, shoved underneath a baseball cap. And she recognized his voice as well . . . except that instead of Chicago-tinged English, he was speaking in fluent Russian.

Barely breathing, she translated the snippets of conversation that she could pick up.

"Rock climbing . . . accident. . . . Things will work out. . . . I understand my orders. . . ."

Sydney let out a gasp. Stephanie was right. Paul was working with K-Directorate. There could be no other explanation for a furtive phone call made in the dark cover of night, in Russian spoken with the ease of a native. And if by some small chance it was a phone call to a friend, Paul would use his cell in front of Maureen, not come all the way up here.

Sydney flattened herself against the kiosk. And then she heard the most chilling words of all, spoken with the cold, hard voice of a killer.

"Don't worry about Stephanie Harling. She will be taken care of."

12

"OKAY, LET'S GO OVER it one more time."
Stephanie took a deep, steadying breath and met
Sydney's eyes in the mirror over the wet paper-
towel-strewn bathroom sink in one of the public
rest rooms across from the falls. They were each
wearing navy blue windbreakers to protect themselves from the perennial wetness, white shorts,
baseball caps, and Nikes. A laptop sat propped up
next to the tiled wall.

Sydney nodded, but she had already committed
the plan they had concocted to memory. As part of
Stephanie and Paul's secret SD-2 mission, Paul was

to pick up a disk from a local informant and then leave that disk for Stephanie in front of a nearby Starbucks. In turn, Stephanie was to give the disk to a bearded man wearing an orange baseball cap on the Whirlpool Aero Car, an aerial cable car that traveled between two points on the Canadian shore of the Niagara River.

"Now, like I've said, I am ninety-nine percent sure that the disk Paul gives me will not be the one he's led me to believe it will be. Instead, it's going to contain secrets vital to SD-2 operations," Stephanie said hurriedly, wringing her hands.

"We'll find out," Sydney said confidently. "I'll get the disk and then run it down to you. You'll be able to do a quick scan on your laptop." If it turned out that Stephanie was wrong, Sydney would go ahead and make the scheduled SD-2 drop as planned. If Stephanie was right, Sydney had given her word that she would help.

Help equaled assistance. Help *didn't* equal kill.

"Right, and meanwhile, I'll be IM'ing Paul's father back at SD-2," Stephanie said calmly, reassuring herself with the details of the plan. "If anything happens to Paul, my online records will prove that I didn't have anything to do with it."

And if things went as she intended, Sydney wouldn't either.

She had made the decision that if Paul was confirmed to be a traitor, she would contact SD-6. Getting involved in a physical altercation with another CIA agent was not something she wanted on her permanent record at SD-6, no matter how justified.

"How do I look?" Sydney asked, adjusting her long blond wig into a loose ponytail and pulling her baseball cap down over her face. In the split second she was going to be near Paul, she was confident he wouldn't detect the switch.

"Like the person who's going to save my life," Stephanie whispered back.

* * *

"That's it," Sydney murmured to herself as she watched Paul Riley put a small black disk on the ledge of an oversized planter outside the busy coffee shop. He casually covered the disk with an empty paper coffee cup and began ambling in her direction, sipping a full cup of coffee.

Five . . . four . . . three . . . two . . . one. Now. She walked briskly toward the familiar Starbucks logo, head down, and as she passed Paul, she gave herself a mental high five. She had learned never to make eye contact with someone when making a drop, and it was likely that Paul followed the same protocol.

If he suspected something, he would most certainly have stopped her.

Pocketing the disk, she walked as quickly as she could down the recreation trail that ran alongside the Niagara Parkway to the entrance of the Whirlpool Aero Car.

"That was fast," Stephanie breathed, stepping out from behind a cluster of trees. She popped open her laptop and Sydney slid the disk into the drive.

She watched over Stephanie's shoulder as Stephanie clicked rapidly through various folders, letting out a low whistle.

Stephanie had been right, and then some. The disk not only gave details of SD-2's operations, but operations of SD-6 and SD-15 as well.

"That bastard," Stephanie hissed.

Sydney couldn't believe what was scrolling down on the laptop screen in front of her. Somehow Paul had gained clearance to Greg's, Maureen's, and Sydney's home offices, downloading complete dossiers on all key staff, along with itemized accounts of all missions and locations of satellite offices. Top-secret information that someone at Sydney's level would never be privy to.

And then Stephanie clicked open a folder that contained a memo:

To: Timothy G.
From: Paul R.
Subject: Agent Stephanie Harling

This memo is to confirm that Stephanie Harling is working against us. Will do what is necessary. Problem will be taken care of before our return from Niagara Falls.

* * *

The red-roofed Aero Car was filled to capacity as it left the disembarking point and began to travel slowly across the turbulent water below. It reminded Sydney of an amusement park sky tram, except much bigger—and with a much scarier view.

Sydney had thought it would be easy to spot her mark, but everyone on board seemed to be wearing a hat, and the crowded car was difficult to navigate. She reached inside her jacket pocket and gave the disk a reassuring touch.

"Excuse me," Sydney said to a large woman busily snapping pictures of her three children posing against the yellow metal railing. Then Sydney spotted a flash of orange. A man with a black goatee, dressed in a jean jacket, jeans, and a trucker-style orange foam hat stood off to the side, barely looking at the water as it formed a massive whirlpool below.

Sydney looked out at the majestic view, trying to calm the pounding in her heart. *Relax. It's not like he's going to know you're tricking him,* she told herself. She took a few photos with the disposable Kodak camera she'd stuck in her pocket for appearance's sake and made a show of pulling out a guide map to the area and studying it closely. Then, after she'd dallied as long as she dared, she nonchalantly walked over to Orange Hat.

As a prerecorded voice detailed the sights below and the *ooh*ing and *ahh*ing Aero Car passengers snapped photographs, Sydney placed the disk on a water-spattered interior ledge, then backed away.

In a split second, Orange Hat had retrieved it.

I wonder what he'll do when he discovers that the intel he was expecting was deleted and replaced with pages of Madame LeFèvre's French vocabulary handouts? Sydney thought, suppressing a chuckle. Stephanie had saved the treasonous information onto her laptop's hard drive; the disk Sydney was handing over would be useless to him.

As the car made its way back to the boarding area and the passengers began to disembark, Sydney watched Orange Hat blend into the crowd.

She agonized over what to do. Should she head

back to the main viewing area to try to find Paul and confront him? She didn't have a weapon, and the thought of getting into a death match with a trained SD officer didn't have a lot of appeal.

And it could be a real death match, she thought uneasily. Because if Paul was ready to hand Stephanie over to K-Directorate on a plate, there was no reason to think he wouldn't just shoot her on sight, especially if he thought she was Stephanie. There was no way to know if the traitorous agent had a gun.

Maybe he did.

Maybe she was in his line of fire right now. Her nerves beginning to fray, she pushed forward through the crowd, not wanting to stand immobile, a potential sitting duck.

As soon as her Nikes hit solid ground, Sydney took off running. "Taxi!" she yelled to an idling city cab at the nearby intersection. "The Horseshoe Falls," she said breathlessly to the driver, climbing into the backseat.

Before she did anything, she would locate Carl Sanderling's notes.

And then I'll call Sloane. Her handler at SD-6 would know exactly what to do.

13

THE SECOND THE ELEVATOR door opened in the Table Rock complex, Sydney jumped out and raced through the empty network of manmade tunnels behind the Horseshoe Falls, her sneakers splashing through puddles. She had been the elevator's sole occupant, and it appeared that she was alone in the tunnel as well. That was good—she didn't have time to explain to any curious bystanders what she was doing. She only had a few minutes to find Sanderling's papers and get back to the main viewing platform, where the agents were to gather for further border patrol instruction.

The tunnel walls were craggy and dank, narrow beams of light making their way through cracks. Sydney pulled out the small flashlight she had in her pocket and clicked it on, then adjusted the tiny earpiece in her right ear. The flashlight beam danced jerkily over the ground as she jogged. Up ahead she could hear the thunder of the falls.

This would be really cool if I weren't working, she thought, coming out onto a small outdoor observation deck that at most could hold three people. Agents were always supposed to tend to the matter at hand, whether they were scaling the Eiffel Tower or walking the Great Wall of China. There wasn't time to be a sightseer.

But sometimes it was hard to follow the rules.

Sydney stopped for a moment, mesmerized by the rush of water. She was far below the rim of the gorge, directly behind the Horseshoe Falls. The platform she was standing on was just above the water level.

Everything she did—school, SD-6, running— seemed so meaningless in the face of such a powerful force of nature. *Insignificant,* she thought, remembering what Stephanie had said on their visit a few days ago. The falls were as thunderous, thrilling, and awesome as she had always imagined them to be.

Brushing back a clump of soggy blond wig, Sydney pulled the bright yellow rain poncho included with the attraction's admission fee around her. In one of its pockets were a magnetic tape measure and a grease pencil, which she used to carefully follow the measurements she'd memorized from Sloane. Sanderling hadn't had time to come up with a complicated hiding place. . . . He had been in fear for his life, and a quickly devised plan to use a crevice in this tunnel made the search not as complicated as it might have been.

"Bluebird. Can you read me?" Graham's voice back in L.A. crackled through her earpiece.

"Copy that," Sydney said, responding to the code name Sloane had asked her to adopt on her missions going forward. "I'm measuring back seven feet from the opening. Go over the dimensions again." She listened as Graham repeated the coordinates to her.

With a steady hand, Sydney positioned the tape measure up the wall, marking off each measurement with her thick orange pencil. When she'd completed the calculations, which took her to a spot precisely at eye level, she took a chisel out of her other pocket and began to chip away at a section of damp rock. According to the calculations, the papers should be . . . there! A large section of rock tumbled to the ground as the flinty crag crumbled to dust beneath her fingers. A small carved-out compartment lay a few inches from her face.

And there, where they had been concealed for over forty years, was a tightly wrapped thick sheath of papers. They were slightly damp and smelled mildewy, but for the most part, they looked fine. It was weird to think that the last person to see them was a man who had died almost fifty years before.

Sydney enjoyed finding things that had been preserved by someone in the past. It was like uncovering a buried treasure, a remnant from another era. Sometimes it felt a bit like invading someone's personal life. . . . She remembered going through her mother's jewelry box after she died, gingerly lifting out necklaces and brooches, knowing that her mother had never imagined she wouldn't come back to her bedroom and wear the beautiful ruby earrings and delicate filigree necklaces once more.

But this isn't anything like that, Sydney thought, carefully removing the papers from their hiding place. Sanderling had hidden his notes because he knew the Russians wanted to use what he had learned about the power of the falls for something he didn't believe in.

"Your notes are safe with me, Mr. Sanderling," Sydney said as she slid them into a waterproof binder.

Sydney kicked the piece of rock that had been covering the hiding place to the side. Then she went back out to the small viewing platform and gazed out at the falls. *Just one more look,* she told herself, understanding how a brilliant man like Carl Sanderling could have become so fascinated with this natural wonder. There was something about the falls that was so powerful, so majestic—

Footsteps echoed down the tunnel. *Perfect timing,* she thought, hoping that no one tripped over the piece of rock. *Explaining why I was gouging out a national Canadian treasure to some tourists from Buffalo isn't on my to-do list today.*

But the person who spoke wasn't a tourist.

"It's over, Stephanie," came the controlled voice of Paul Riley. Sydney kept her head down, her face shielded by her baseball cap and poncho hood. "And seeing you here, doing—Well, this confirms it. I'm sorry it has to be this way."

"So am I," Sydney said, gritting her teeth. "Unhh!" Her roundhouse kick knocked a startled Paul off his feet.

In a flash, he was back up. His Topsiders, jeans, and rain poncho gave him the look of a college student, but his body language told her he probably knew a thing or two about martial arts.

She jumped back, readying her stance. She didn't need to look around to know that there was nowhere to go. The route back to the top was blocked. Behind her was the small observation deck overlooking the thundering water of Niagara.

In front of her was a traitorous combat-trained agent, ready to kill.

"Think about what you're doing!" she warned, wondering if there was any way she could diffuse the situation. She went to pull off her wig, but before she could do it, Paul yanked her arm hard, sending her to the ground. She leaped up before he could stop her, kicking him deep in the ribs. He spun around, barely fazed.

Sydney was a good, strong fighter, but after several minutes of intense sparring, she knew she was outmatched. With his size and experience, Paul was better and stronger. If only she could get to the elevator, she'd have a fighting chance. Because here on the small platform, she had two opponents: Paul and the churning water that surrounded them.

"Bluebird! Bluebird!" Graham's distraught voice buzzed in her ear. "Are you all right?"

But there was nothing anyone back at SD-6 could do for her now. She was on her own.

Suddenly she felt Paul's fist punch her in the stomach. She gasped, momentarily incapacitated. "No!" Sydney screamed a second later as Paul used his trump card to twist her left arm behind her, pinning it to her back.

Her feet scrambled on the wet slate floor, trying to gain a foothold. Paul shoved her backward, and her body pressed against the cold, hard railing. *Does he wonder why it's me instead of Stephanie?* she wondered as her eyes caught his. She recognized the look on his face, and it scared her. It was the same look she had worn when she had been kicking some serious enemy butt on a mission. A look of pumped-up adrenaline, fueled by the heat of the fight.

Except she *wasn't* the enemy. *Or maybe I am,* she thought as he shoved her again and her head snapped back, her baseball cap plunging into the water and foam splashing her face. While Paul was a traitor to the United States, Sydney believed in everything the CIA stood for—and she'd made that very clear during their training. *I'm just one more obstacle in his way.*

Only several feet separated them from the roaring water below. People came to this spot for a safe thrill and amazing view, to feel the mist on their faces and get as close to Niagara Falls as they could without being in real danger.

Not to die.

With the roar of the falls and Graham's nervous outburst ringing in her ears, Sydney struggled, her poncho making squeaking noises as it chafed against the railing. She tried every defense tactic she could think of, but Paul was too quick. He blocked her attempt to knee him in the groin and left no part of himself open to attack.

After several seconds of intense struggle, Paul reached his left hand around Sydney's throat, his fingers squeezing hard. *He's going to strangle me!* Sydney thought in a panic as her eyes blinked out rapid tears. The sound of the water was deafening. Blood rushed to Sydney's head as her neck fell farther back, her long blond hair dangling over the water.

She tried to reach up and peel his fingers off, but she was losing strength—and hope—fast. *I can't die like this!* she thought as hysteria swept over her. If she was able to get away, she could dive into the water, but that was almost a certain death. No swimmer, no matter how strong, could survive under such powerful pressure.

Sydney gulped for air as her attacker wrapped both of his hands more tightly around her neck, shaking her. He pushed her against the slick wet railing, and it groaned with their weight. A half-formed sob came out as Sydney realized she had only a handful of seconds of air left. Soon she would be unconscious.

Then he'll toss me like a doll into the rapids. . . .

* * *

"Hey. Hey!" Someone was screaming at them. At first Sydney thought it was someone behind her, swimming in the water, but that was impossible. Her vision blurred as she made out a figure standing on the wet platform above them, wildly waving its arms. *Stephanie,* Sydney thought thickly as her friend pulled her hooded raincoat down, revealing herself. "Let Sydney go!" she shrieked to Paul over the thrashing torrent of water. "I'm the one you want!"

Paul turned a wild eye to Sydney, as if truly seeing who she was for the first time. For a moment she thought he was going to kill her anyway. Then she was sucking in air as his fingers loosened their grip on her neck and he stumbled away, drawing the back of his hand across his mouth. Choking, she slumped against the water-slicked railing, gasping for breath, the sound of Paul's footsteps racing back to the elevator pounding in her skull.

14

AS SOON AS SHE had regained her breath, Sydney raced for the elevator, counting the seconds until the doors opened and she could scramble inside. When it deposited her on the upper level, Sydney burst out, looking wildly around her for a sign of Stephanie or Paul. Taking in the confused faces of tourists lining the outside walkway, she jogged by them, her sneakers squishing water as she ran.

Up ahead, there was a mini-commotion going on. "He almost knocked me down!" a woman with frizzy red hair and a bright blue tube top was loudly complaining to her bewildered husband. His pudgy stature showed that he was in no condition to do anything about this.

"Which way did he go?" Sydney blurted out, certain that the woman could only be talking about Paul.

"Down there," the woman huffed, pointing a red painted fingernail at a figure running toward the *Maid of the Mist* entrance. "You give him a piece of my mind! Creep."

Sydney ran down the sidewalk, quickly paid the admission fee, then flew down the ramp that led to the departure area, bumping into a few people herself. A bank of elevators took visitors down to the base of the falls, and Sydney jostled to be in the front, ignoring the annoyed stares of the tourists around her.

When the elevator opened, she accepted a poncho from a staff member and then was outside once more. She immediately scrutinized the crowd boarding the *Maid of the Mist*. The boat looked much larger up close. In the few seconds it had taken her to get there, Paul had blended in with the throng of tourists jockeying for a spot on the watercraft. Her eyes scanned the people on the boat's crowded deck. Everyone was wearing the regulation *Maid of the Mist* blue plastic hooded rain ponchos, making each passenger virtually indistinguishable from another.

There she is! she thought, elated to see Stephanie's long blond hair whipping in the wind. The *Maid of the Mist* was just starting to pull away from the dock. Sydney could hear a tinny-sounding audio begin its spiel. If Stephanie had managed to board and strand Paul on land, Sydney could call in for backup. She'd have no problem keeping him contained in this area.

But it was too late. Sydney's eyes lit on the tall figure of Paul Riley, his hood pushed off his blond head and a determined expression fixed on his lips. She watched in horror as he began cutting his way through the crowd toward Stephanie.

"Let me through!" Sydney cried to a cluster of tourists who had missed the departure.

"The line's back there," a man said angrily, pointing his thumb back toward the snaking line of people.

"But—" she began helplessly as the *Maid of the Mist* moved farther into the water. "I have to get on that boat!"

"Welcome to the *Maid of the Mist*, one of North America's most famous tourist attractions!" came a perky voice over the boat's loudspeaker. "For your safety, please hold young children by the hand, and please do not hang over the railings. We will be—"

"You don't understand," Sydney said to the group at large, her heart thumping wildly. "This is a matter of life and death!"

The people around her rolled their eyes, then resumed their conversations.

"There's more than one boat," a kind-looking woman spoke up, tapping her on the shoulder. "The next one should be here in, oh, ten minutes or so. You'll make that one for sure."

Sydney tried to smile, but she was in a panic. There was a good chance that Stephanie would die if she couldn't come up with a way to get on the *Maid of the Mist* that had just disembarked. Overwhelmed with frustration, she ripped off her poncho and shook it out over the concrete ground. A jumble of Graham's gadgets fell out of its pockets—the leather gloves with the digital camera, the tube of lipstick, and the waterproof laser wristwatch.

Sydney stood there dripping, staring down helplessly at the gadgets. She was paralyzed with indecision. Every second that passed put Paul another inch closer to harming Stephanie, but Sydney couldn't think straight. How could she help?

A humming in her ear jolted her back.

"Graham!" she cried with relief, startling several passers-by with her outburst. For once, the sound of static was a welcome noise. She *wasn't* completely alone. Graham was a certified genius—maybe *he* could think of something.

Sydney took a deep breath. "There's an enemy agent on a boat going toward the base of the falls, and I need to stop him," she said quickly. "Is there anything I have that can help me?"

Silence. Then Graham began, "Well, let's see. Okay. Um, well, you know, uh, you have the poncho—"

"Yes," Sydney said.

"It's bulletproof—"

"Yes!" Sydney said, trying not to let her impatience get the best of her. "Graham, tell me something I *don't* know!"

"It would take a stack of three million two thousand dimes to reach the top of the Empire State Building," Graham said, suppressing a nervous chuckle. "Ha ha. Okay, back to the matter at hand. You, uh, have the digital camera gloves—"

Sydney fell to her knees and picked them up. She flipped the gloves over, not sure what they could do for her.

"Well, see, there isn't exactly a camera inside them," he said as her fingers hurriedly smoothed over the soft thick black leather. "Instead—"

Wham! Sydney reared back in surprise as her fingers pressed a tiny bump on the inside wristband. A thin black nylon cord sprang out from the palm of the glove, à la the Spider-Man-web gloves she'd played with as a child. The cord had a round black tip that had adhered to the damp pavement, and when she tugged it, it felt strong as steel.

"The glitch," she whispered, pushing on the palm of the gloves again. The cord zinged back into its hiding place.

"How long is the cord?" she asked breathlessly.

"I'm going to say nine hundred feet, but it could be eight hundred. Or it could be a thousand," Graham said into her earpiece. "There were several pairs of these gloves made, and none of them have uniformity in the length of—"

Sydney didn't need to hear any more. Hope surged through her as she jammed the lipstick and watch into her pocket. She leaped to her feet and dashed to the safety railing that was the closest spot on land to the boat. With lightning speed, she unsnapped the small black band at the top of the right glove, wrapped it around the rail, and fastened it in place. "Let's hope Graham used industrial-strength snaps on these things," she muttered, giving the glove a test tug.

"Syd? Did you call me? What are you doing?" Graham asked worriedly. "Sydney, if you're doing what I think you're doing—"

Sydney crouched down so she was eye level with the railing. The *Maid of the Mist* bobbed several hundred yards in front of her, its diesel engine churning up water. "Let's cross our fingers for one thousand," she mumbled as she aimed the tiny opening for the cord at the boat.

She held her breath as she pushed down on the concealed button. *Whizz!* The cord shot out and, to her amazement, hit the boat directly above its *Maid of the Mist III* logo on the bow.

"Score!" she exhaled excitedly under her breath.

"No! Don't use them. It's a glitch!" Graham screamed in Sydney's earpiece as she tossed her poncho aside and wiped her sweaty palms on her shorts legs. "They haven't been safety tested!"

The boat continued to move toward the base of the American Falls, its red and white Canadian flag whipping smartly in the breeze off the stern. If the boat moved too far away, the cord would snap loose. Sydney had to be fast. And she had to be fearless. *Don't look down,* she ordered herself, remembering Greg's words from their rock-climbing expedition. *Whatever you do, don't look down!* But she didn't have to see the rushing water to know it was there—the thundering power of the falls was deafening.

With a gulp, Sydney climbed over the railing and secured herself as best as she could on the cord. *Why didn't I think to ask Graham how much weight the cord can hold?* she thought, fear swimming in her blood as a small crowd of horrified onlookers gathered onshore and a panicked staff member got on his cell phone. Well, it was too late now. Squeezing her eyes shut, she began to slither down the slick cord feetfirst toward the boat.

It had only taken a few seconds for the splashing water below to completely soak her. She clung to the cord with both hands, her feet wrapped tightly around the bottom. Moving first her right hand, then her left, Sydney inched her way down its length, moving her torso and legs last. Thankfully the cord remained taut. Each movement brought her closer to the boat . . . and to the water below.

You're almost there. You're almost there, Sydney mentally repeated to herself, the mantra helping keep her wits about her as her back hung suspended mere feet away from almost certain death. People had survived this and much worse in a barrel, for heaven's sake. She didn't have one of those, but she *was* a trained CIA officer. That ought to count for something, right?

She tried to think of the cord as a rope in gym class. Sure. The only difference was, this rope was slick with sea spray—and letting go meant more than a fall on a padded mat.

"Unhhh!" Sydney clung for her life as the boat made an unexpected—at least to her—turn, and the cord swung wildly. She blinked quickly, momentarily blinded by the powerful spray. *How much farther?* she wondered in frustration, trying not to think about the terrifying rapids below.

Move it, Bristow! she told herself, trying not to cry. If Noah were here, he'd tell her to do her job and do it now. *And I'd listen,* Sydney thought sternly, the idea of looking pathetic in front of Noah Hicks a fate worse than death. Thinking of him spurred her on, and soon she was able to make out the confused faces of the *Maid of the Mist* passengers.

Sydney's arms were shaking with fatigue, and tiny rivulets of blood ran from the palms of her hands from where she gripped the cord. And then, for what seemed like the first time in hours, she heard the sound of another human being.

Someone on the boat was screaming.

Stephanie.

The sound filled her with adrenalized energy, and in a few seconds she was at the edge of the boat. With a final thrust, Sydney hoisted herself on board. She dropped with an unceremonious thud on the wet deck. Seconds later the cord broke off as the boat drifted out of range toward the American Falls.

I did it! she thought, overwhelmed with the accomplishment. Her legs quivered beneath her. But there was no time for a mental pat on the back.

Taking a second to get her bearings, Sydney immediately spotted Stephanie and Paul. The two agents were having an out-and-out war on the steps that led to the boat's upper level. Frightened tourists in rain ponchos were hurriedly shoving each other to get out of their way.

"Stay out of this," Paul snarled over his shoulder at Sydney. He had cornered Stephanie at the prow of the boat. His blond hair was stuck in wet clumps on his forehead, and his face was flushed red with anger. In his hands was an oar, which he menaced in front of Stephanie.

Stephanie's face was white. "Please, don't do this. I—"

Wham! Before Sydney could make a move, Paul smashed the oar into the side of Stephanie's head. She crumpled like a rag doll onto the steps.

"Stephanie!" Sydney gasped, stepping toward

her. Then she darted quickly back as Paul turned toward her. Anger surged through her chilled veins. She'd already had one battle with Paul that afternoon. *A battle I would have lost if he hadn't gone after Stephanie.*

There was no way she could back down now. But how was she going to win?

The watch! Sydney had forgotten all about the watch! She pulled it out of her pocket, aimed it at Paul, and then pushed the hand.

Paul let out a cry, then slumped over.

"Graham, you really had my back on this one," she said as she took down a piece of rope from the side of the boat and began expertly binding Paul's hands together. She had five minutes before the laser wore off.

"Who *are* you?" asked two middle-school-age girls who had been anxiously watching the whole thing, raising their voices to be heard over the falls. "You're either a superhero or really bad, and we can't tell which."

"I'm a good guy," Sydney promised, smiling up at them. "If I had my badge with me, I'd show you. And if you want to help me, go find some more rope." Sydney used the rope she had left to tie Paul's feet together. He wasn't completely secured—she'd need a few feet more to be safe.

Leaving Paul where he was, Sydney ran over to a glass-enclosed area, where a man she assumed was the captain stood inside. She banged on the glass. He held what appeared to be a walkie-talkie up to his mouth. He looked very upset.

"Turn this boat around!" Sydney ordered, water streaming down her face. "I am a federal agent!"

The captain didn't move. Instead, he glared at her through the smudged glass. "Yeah, and I'm Brad Pitt. Listen, young lady, you have put this boat and the hundreds of passengers who are on it in terrible danger!" he scolded. "We are finishing our course, which will take approximately ten more minutes to navigate."

"We don't have ten minutes!" Sydney pointed frantically back at Paul. "See that guy over there? When he wakes up, and he will, in, oh, two minutes, your boat is going to be in *serious* danger."

"And when we finish our course," the captain said, ignoring her, "the United States Coast Guard and Canadian police will be escorting you and your friends off my boat."

"I'm going to be escorting *you* into the falls if you don't divert this boat!" Sydney yelled, giving the glass a frustrated slap. Obviously she wasn't getting anywhere with him. She decided to turn her attention to her fellow passengers.

All of them looked terrified.

The two young girls were nowhere to be found—and neither was their rope. Sydney glanced up and saw Paul stirring slightly. "Get me some more rope!" she barked to a bewildered group of German tourists, using their native tongue. As they scurried off, she waved her hands at a couple that was peering curiously at Paul. "Stay away from him!"

By this point, no one was paying any attention to the canned voice-over, which still continued to extol the virtues of the falls, complete with stories of daredevil rescues. The show on the boat was much more interesting.

"We found this," one of the young girls said, suddenly appearing in front of her. She held out a jump rope. "It was in my little brother's backpack."

"This will do just fine," Sydney said, turning toward Paul.

But he was gone.

Some misguided Good Samaritan had untied Paul's hands, and when the stun gun had worn off, he had hobbled over to Stephanie. He loomed over her now, his feet still loosely bound.

Sydney watched in horror as he gathered Stephanie in his arms, then glanced up at the roaring American Falls. Paul was going to throw her overboard!

"No!" Sydney cried. She grabbed a blue and white life preserver and slid across the boat toward him. The boat pitched forward and Sydney rammed into Paul full force.

"Holy—" Paul screeched as the body slam knocked him into the railing. He tossed Stephanie aside and raised his fist to punch Sydney in the face.

Without a moment's hesitation, Sydney clutched the life preserver and walloped him in the gut with every ounce of strength she had. This was one fight she had to win. He stumbled back, his feet still bound, and she whacked him with the preserver again. But this time he didn't just stumble backward.

He toppled over the edge of the boat.

Sydney gaped in disbelief as Paul clung to the front railing of the *Maid of the Mist,* his fingers clutching desperately to the cold, wet metal. His eyes bore into hers. Cold, angry, frightened eyes.

Should I grab his hand and help him back up? Sydney wondered in a daze, not sure how to react. But that would be too risky. He was likely to pull *her* over if she did that. Next to her, Stephanie let out a groggy moan.

"Somebody do something!" someone cried behind her. Several passengers gasped. But this time no Good Samaritans stepped forward.

"Man overboard! Man overboard!" shouted the captain over the loudspeaker.

And then, in slow motion, Sydney watched in dismay as Agent Paul Riley's fingers slid off the railing, and he plummeted silently into the thundering water of Niagara Falls.

![15]

THE BOAT LOOKED LIKE a child's bathtub toy
from where Sydney and Stephanie stood on the
main viewing area of the Niagara Parkway. Helicopters swarmed overhead, and a few hundred
yards away sat two parked ambulances, their lights
whirring. Policemen bustled importantly around
them, speaking brusquely into walkie-talkies.

"That is some goose egg," Sydney said, cau-
tiously touching the large tender lump that had
formed on Stephanie's forehead. "You've got to see
a doctor immediately."

"I will," Stephanie said, flinching. "Believe me, my head has seen worse."

They were quiet for a moment, the buzz of the helicopters drowning out their voices.

"I still can't believe we slipped away," Stephanie said, staring down at the water. In the confusion after Paul had gone overboard, the distraught captain had quickly returned the boat to the departure dock. Sydney had roused Stephanie and the two of them had managed to flee the area undetected. They'd quickly purchased souvenir T-shirts and cheap sunglasses, ditching their soaked clothes in a Dumpster behind the visitors' center. Now they easily blended in with the confused crowd of onlookers gaping down at the accident scene below.

"I can't believe he tried to kill me," Sydney said, reaching up to rub her sore neck. Her body felt bruised and beaten, but for the most part, she was okay. "The look in his eyes—" She broke off, not sure what was the right thing to say. After all, her friend had just lost someone who had at one time meant a great deal to her—not to mention someone who had once been a trusted fellow agent.

Stephanie reached over and squeezed Sydney's hand. "I can't thank you enough for what you just did, Sydney. You saved my life." A tear slipped down her cheek. "It's just so hard to believe that he hated me that much. Enough to want to kill me. And you."

Sydney squeezed Stephanie's hand back. "I don't think it was you he hated, Stephanie. Paul was a traitor to the CIA and to the United States. And you were the one unlucky enough to catch him. You're the one the agency should be proud of."

Sydney's initial shock at watching Paul plunge to almost-certain death had been replaced by resolute acceptance. There was no doubt in her mind that he had caused his own death. He was a traitor. And she was an agent of the CIA, doing her job.

Well, it wasn't exactly an official assignment, her nagging conscience reminded her. SD-6 hadn't sanctioned today's events—they didn't even know about them. Graham only had a few kernels of information—and after calling in on a borrowed cell phone to assure him that she was okay, Sydney had decided not to give him any more. Why get more people involved than she needed to? She would let her handler know that she had assisted an agent from SD-2 on a mission while she was in Niagara Falls, and if Sloane wanted to follow up with Stephanie's handler at SD-2, that was his business.

I've done nothing wrong, she told herself firmly, watching as the rescue boats navigated the choppy water in search of Paul's body. She looked over at Stephanie. For the first time in days, her friend's body language looked relaxed. *In fact, I did everything right.*

"So, I'm going to do it," Stephanie blurted out, her chin jutting outward defiantly. "I'm going to enter the witness protection program the higher-ups at SD-2 have offered me. Not even Paul's father will know where I am."

"But—but you're such a good agent," Sydney protested as they sat down on a newly vacated bench. "The Agency *needs* people like you. People who care."

Stephanie shook her head. "I've cared enough to last a lifetime." She scuffed the ground with her still-damp shoe. "Nope, I'm ready to leave my SD-2 days behind me. Do something completely normal, like become a manager at Banana Republic. Great discounts on cashmere sweaters, I hear." Stephanie laughed. "Or who knows? Maybe I really will look for a job in insurance." Then she grew quiet. "Be somebody who can look her roommates in the eye and tell them the truth about what I do for a living. Look myself in the eye too."

Sydney bit her lip. When the CIA had first recruited her back in September, she had been filled with doubt. With her genius-level IQ, her predilection for languages, and her natural interest in government and history, she had been an obvious candidate for the CIA. Obvious to everyone but her. Becoming a CIA officer had never occurred to her as a career choice until Wilson had approached her that day in the quad, handing over his business card.

Now, all these months later, despite all the danger and potential anguish, despite all the lies to the people she cared about, Sydney couldn't imagine a life without SD-6. She told lies, to be sure, but she told them for a very good reason: they protected her loved ones. They were necessary.

As was SD-6. It had given her life a purpose.

And for that, she'd be eternally grateful.

"I hope you aren't getting any ideas about quitting your day job," Stephanie said suddenly, her timing making Sydney blink in surprise. "Because seeing you in action—you are one incredible agent. How you climbed down that cord onto the boat—" She shook her head in disbelief. "That was totally amazing. I hope you guys get a patent on that thing."

"I have to give credit to Graham back at HQ," Sydney said, wishing Graham could have seen his devices in action. Maybe someday. She grinned. "Don't worry. I might have gotten a bit shaken up out there today, but I have no intention of leaving

SD-6." She shrugged. "It's weird, but it's in my blood."

Stephanie leaned over and gave her an impulsive hug. "I'll never forget you, Sydney," she said softly. "You were a real friend to me today."

Sydney hugged her back, a lump forming in her throat at the thought of saying good-bye. She hadn't been a friend to Stephanie just for today.

She would be her friend forever.

16

A RUSH OF COOL air greeted Sydney as she pulled open the dorm door, wheeling her suitcase behind her, and walked into the lobby. Brightly colored advertisements for used books and announcements for events that had long since passed still hung haphazardly on the bulletin board, and a tired-looking janitor was pushing the furniture to the walls as he prepared to mop the residence hall floor.

Except for a guy Sydney didn't know walking by listening to his Discman, it was deserted. It was obviously very different here at UCLA during the summer session. Gone was the hustle and bustle of people on their way to class or the gym or, on a good day, the beach. No clusters of students were hanging out in front of the coffee cart, which was closed; no music was playing; and the smell of popcorn that inevitably was being popped somewhere in the high-rise had been replaced by lemon-scented cleaning solution.

As she waited for the elevator doors to open, Sydney felt a tingle of the old familiar dread. Back to UCLA meant back to lying. Back to trying to cover up every time SD-6 called her with an urgent mission. She hoped she could still do it. Lie, that was. Now that she was home, she couldn't hide her emotions so easily. Francie could always tell in an instant when something was terribly wrong just by looking at Sydney's face.

The elevator doors opened and Sydney stepped inside. *Duh. Francie's not going to be here.* She was out in New Mexico solving some major crisis like mopping up spilled apple juice or regulating how many Elmo videos her young charges could watch before the entire family, including Francie, went crazy.

When the elevator arrived on her floor, Sydney walked down the empty hallway, past an occasional gum wrapper and a few crumpled-up flyers. The air inside her room felt hot and stuffy, and she flipped the air-conditioning on high, then kicked off her shoes and sat down heavily on her bed.

The room looked exactly the same. Same minifridge. Same woolly cream-colored Pottery Barn rug she and Francie had selected together. Same stack of used textbooks on her desk. Same string of jalapeño lights Francie had strewn across her side of the room. Same James Dean poster. Same campus view out of the same dusty windows.

Sydney sighed.

And the same lonely girl.

After taking a long, hot shower, Sydney put on a clean pair of shorts and a white tank top and slipped on a pair of flip-flops. She combed her wet hair behind her ears and dabbed on some gel in hopes that it would stay that way. Then she put on a light coat of mascara, dusted some blush across her cheekbones, and stuck her sunglasses and her wallet in her leather satchel.

After all the planes, taxis, and harrowing boat rides, it was going to feel great to get behind the wheel of her Mustang and be in control. It was going to feel even better once she reached the beach and felt the warm sand under her toes and the late June afternoon sunshine on her face.

Sydney pulled the door shut behind her and reached in her satchel for her cell phone. There was just one phone call she was going to have to make before she reached her destination.

Maybe she wouldn't have to be a lonely girl forever.

*   *   *

"So . . . I thought you were in Asia," Sydney said to Noah Hicks two hours later. They sat side by side, shoulders almost touching, on a faded floral blanket on the sand, the surf crashing a hundred yards in front of them. Most of the beachgoers had packed up for the day, leaving only a few random Frisbee players and a couple of dog walkers to enjoy what Sydney considered the best part of the day to be at the beach.

She toyed with the fringe on the blanket, not meeting his gaze. He had met her there, no questions asked, an hour after she had phoned, which was something considering L.A. traffic. Knowing that made her happier than she could have predicted.

"Then why did you call?" Noah asked, looking over at her. His straight hair was tousled and the small lines around his eyes crinkled in the sun. Noah looked like a normal guy at the beach with his faded khaki shorts and navy Abercrombie shirt . . .

except Sydney was convinced that *normal* and *Noah* didn't belong in the same sentence.

Why *had* she called him? That was a good question. The truth was that from the time she had stood with Stephanie at the top of the falls, the helicopters swarming overhead as Paul Riley's lifeless body was pulled from the water, to the moment her plane had landed at LAX, the only person Sydney had wanted to see was Noah.

Not that she was going to tell *him* that.

Sydney had learned something on this trip. Something more than how to scale a wall, debug a room, and conjugate verbs in French. For the first time, she really, truly understood that everyone— everyone at SD-6, SD-2, SD-5, whatever—had a hidden, secret life.

Did it matter that she had been told Noah was in Asia when he actually was going to happy hours in Marina del Rey? Or did she need to grill him to find out that he *had* gone to Asia but had returned ahead of schedule?

Or does it simply matter that I had someone to call—and that he showed up when I did?

No one in Sydney's personal life knew about SD-6—not her professors, not Todd, not Francie. *Not even my dad!* Noah didn't know about Burke. . . . At least, she didn't think so, and if he did, he didn't know much. Emily Sloane didn't know about her husband's real world. Sydney hadn't known that her former handler, Wilson, had been a traitor to their country.

As she wiggled her toes into the sand, Sydney decided that she didn't need to tell Sloane or Noah or *anyone* at SD-6 what had happened between Stephanie and Paul.

It was over. She knew in her heart that she had done the right thing. She had handled it professionally, as expected of someone in her position at SD-6.

And, her brain reiterated, it was over.

"Sometimes you do things in this job that surprise you," Noah said out of the blue.

Sydney gaped at him. It was as if he could read her mind.

"Don't be so hard on yourself, Sydney," Noah said, his fingertips grazing her bare shoulders. "You're definitely Herculean, but you aren't strong enough to carry the weight of the world." He lightly kissed her collarbone, sending a tiny shiver down her spine. "Besides, these shoulders are much too attractive for that."

"I don't know what's going on, but somehow you are saying all the right things today," Sydney said, letting her head rest against Noah's shoulder.

She breathed in his soapy, musky smell as the beach slowly began to darken into twilight.

Noah leaned into her. "I might not always *say* the right things, but it's not because I don't know what they are, Syd."

Sydney had never been quite sure what she and Noah had together. But whatever it was, it felt good.

For a moment, a brief moment, she let herself think about Paul Riley one final time. She had watched a fellow human being die. A bad guy, to be sure. But, still . . .

Had Noah ever had to kill someone? Did she really want to know?

No, I don't think I do, she thought contentedly as Noah slipped his hand over her own, his fingers twining with hers.

Holding hands with Noah felt good. Really good. And if it ended up turning into something more than that, that would be good too. Really good.

But for now, being honest with herself was the only thing Sydney knew for sure that she could ever, really, hold on to.

I am saddened to report the death of agent Paul Rzhevsky. He had successfully integrated himself into the culture of SD-2 in Chicago and was about to bring in one of its most cunning agents, an S. Harling.

He will be missed.

To: bossman@creditdauphine.com

From:
stephanie.harling@peerless.com

Subject: Sydney Bristow

Dear Agent Sloane,

I am very pleased to report that
my training mission has been
one hundred percent successful.
Not only is Sydney Bristow
completely loyal to SD-6, she
possesses tactical skills well
beyond those of most agents in
the field. I have been able to
verify her involvement with
Agent Noah Hicks in the SD-6
office, but I am confident that
he will not be an issue in her
development as an agent.

Sir, I must commend you on your
recruitment of what is sure to
be one of the finest recruits

SD-6 has ever had in its ranks.
I look forward to continuing my
work in Chicago and hope to
see you when you are in town.

Most sincerely,
Stephanie A. Harling